Mistaken Identity

Sylvia Hubbard

http://SylviaHubbard.com

Mistaken Identity Synopsis:

Mistaken Identity is about a woman who finds inner strength being someone else, but may be the fool in the end for her deceit.

Author's Note:

I started Mistaken Identity from a wedding prompt given by my writing buddy LaDonna in her Yahoo group called Too Sexy For You Writers.

The prompt had to contain a sex scene and a wedding scene. I produced a short story. Everyone enjoyed it so much and demanded a part two.

By the end of that, I was getting threats for my life and decided to produce a blog so everyone could read the story.

I've also been asked who was my inspiration for the male character. I'm embarrassed to admit that it was Jerome Bettis. After getting the writing prompt, I was flipping through a magazine and I saw a big picture of him and I just couldn't get him out of my head. My fantasies started to evolve into a story and bam! Jerome Lott appeared. Thank you Tracey Bettis for giving me your blessing to use your brother, LOL, and not minding.

Special thanks also goes out to Octavia Lesley, who was a very supportive writing friend on the last leg of this publishing journey.

Your Author,

Sylvia Hubbard

Enjoy...

Mistaken Identity

Mistaken Identity © Jan 2006 Sylvia M. Hubbard

Edited by: Moyna Uddin

Cover design by Sylvia Hubbard

ISBN: 0-9774435-1-5

For information address:

http://HubBooks.biz

Sylvia Hubbard

PO Box 27310, Detroit, MI 48227

Visit her website at:

http://SylviaHubbard.com

To schedule this author for events or speaking engagements, please contact: hubbooks@yahoo.com or call 313.289.8614

MISTAKEN IDENTITY

By

Sylvia Hubbard

To the best writing buddy and friend a writer/mother/woman could ever have. (And the best organizer – in life and business, that I've ever known.) I'm so glad to have you apart of my life, LaDonna Tutt!

Part 1

"Lonely Ass Bitch!" shrilled her drunken twin sister, Denise, at least twice last night so everyone could hear at her bachelorette party.

Of course, Dana couldn't fault her sister for her verbal lashing. For some reason, despite Denise's success in her personal life that Dana felt she would never accomplish, Denise was always venomously jealous of Dana for having a great business life. Or at least that is what Dana thought her sister hated her for.

Dana had opted to drop out of college in her third year just shy of twenty credits to her bachelors to open up her own medical billing office. Denise had stayed in school, met Jerome Lott, who was the all-star quarterback from a Detroit high school and had become second round draft pick for the Detroit Lions. Motown had been the city where Denise and Dana had grown up and gone to school, but not the same school as Jerome's. Matter-of-fact, he had attended the rival high school in Detroit.

Denise was now living pretty in her expensive home out in the boondocks of Michigan, while Dana was still living in the side by side two family flat that she owned all alone, but making a very comfortable living for herself. With her office space on one side and her living quarters on the other side, she lived quite well – all alone.

Dana was never a good people person. Denise was definitely the social butterfly of the two. She flitted around and became popular wherever they went, while Dana had a hard time just making simply eye contact with others.

So today – which was Denise's wedding day; Dana sat in the corner of her sister's expansive master bedroom, watching her sister bitch and cry about her hangover from last night's party. Her maidens in waiting – mostly sorority sisters – babied and coddled her.

No one really paid attention to Dana, who was dressed in the ugly lime green dress that the maid of honor was assigned to wear. Denise's colors for the wedding were white and gold. Dana knew the only reason she had been given the position of maid of honor was because their mother had ordered it.

Denise could care less if her own twin sister was a part of the ceremony or not.

"Fuck it!" Denise screamed. "Get this damn dress off me now!"

Everyone, except Dana tried to persuade her not to do this, but Denise's shallow mind was made up and she began to almost rip the dress off her body until her best friend, Gloria, came up and unzipped it for her.

Dana bit her lip and watched as her sister angrily ran out the room, in a camisole bra, panties, and stocking. Denise had always been high strung and most likely would need either a "pick me up," to get her nerves in check or a large gallon of vodka.

Either or wouldn't matter to Denise, who was often termed the life of the party once she had two or three drinks in her.

Everyone, except Dana, followed her sister out leaving Dana in the room by herself. The ceremony wasn't due to start for another hour and most likely; Denise was just using the last of her time to cry for the attention she loved to have.

Dana went over to the door and locked it. The ceremony was taking place in the back yard at the home Jerome had bought for his soon to be wife and the only one with a key would be Denise or Jerome, but he wasn't even here. He had stayed at the hotel for the past three weeks because Denise wanted to "keep him away," while close family and friends were coming into town as if they had not been fucking like rabbits for the past five years. Denise loved to make people think she was always the good girl.

Maybe because Dana had always really been the one. Dana was no virgin, but she had always been selective about who she choose to open her legs to. For the past year, Denise had tried to get information out of Dana about who was "her first," but Dana had kept that information to herself. That was none of anyone's business and if the boy was not talking, then neither would Dana.

When she was positive she could hear her sister screaming for attention downstairs, Dana went over to the gorgeous wedding dress and picked it up. Quickly, without another thought, she pulled off her lime green dress and put on the beautiful ivory and pearl creation.

She knew she would never have another opportunity like this again and she didn't want it to pass.

It fit perfectly. Well it should. They were twins and the only thing that separated them was their personalities. For one day, Dana would have loved to become "Denise." Just take what she wanted, live how she wanted, and behave without rules or morals –

The door opened suddenly and she turned to stare straight into Jerome's face. He was dressed in his tuxedo and fuck if he didn't look damn good from head to toe. Thick wide shoulders, six feet seven, thick powerful thighs, long legs, big feet, and a flawless brownish-red complexion. He was freshly shaven and shorn. For an instant, Dana longed to run her fingertips across his glistening baldhead.

"Damn! Denise," he hissed, closing and locking the door. "You look gorgeous."

Before she could admit the truth, he seemed to leap across the massive room and sweep her up into his arms - Big powerful arms with large hands that seemed everywhere at once. His tongue entwined in hers and he tasted like dark chocolate and peppermint.

'Just for a second, Dana,' she told herself responding just as passionate as he.

Despite the dress' layers she the pressure of his shaft as he pressed against her and she knew that his big feet represented a lot more than his body's size. Instantly, her pussy was wet and she was reminded that she hadn't had any in a very long time.

He broke the kiss suddenly. "Fuck a wait, D. Okay?"

Every time she attempted to protest, his juicy soft lips nibbled, suckled and licked every objection into welcomed silence. Soon his tongue was back down her throat and he was removing the dress with a tenderness that amazed her. He tossed his jacket to the floor and before she knew it his pants were down to his knees.

'Two more minutes, Dana, and then stop and tell him the truth,' she told herself, running her hands over this bald scalp loving the feel of it against her palm. Quickly, she unbuttoned his shirt as he sucked her neck. She was certain the evidence of their encounter would be strawberry red in the morning, dammit she didn't care and worse – she wanted more.

He gently pulled her bra straps down as his mouth found a hardened nipple and sucked it as if milk were about to burst forth.

'Shit! Damn!' her mind silently cursed as she bit her lip to fight the urge to speak and give away her identity.

He stepped out his pants and carried her to the bed, his mouth still attached to her breast and when her back touched the silk duvet cover he was over her, continuing his plight down to where her passion was overflowing.

His hands moved between her thighs and one of his thick digits pressed past her panties and into her heaven.

"Fuck, D. You're so wet. You've never been this damn wet before," he chuckled triumphantly as he removed his finger and nosily sucked it as his other hand pulled his throbbing member free of his mesh briefs.

She sat up, not wanting him to get a good look at her face, but he wasn't interested in looking at her face because his face followed his hands again as he pushed her panties out the way and his strapping tongue lavished her with some special attention that she had not gotten in almost a decade. *'Oh damn! Oh damn!'* she thought as fireworks exploded in her head.

When his face appeared again, his deep almond-shaped eyes were glistening with passion and her love juices. Just as he rose to climb atop the bed, she slid toward his torso and engulfed him deep in her mouth.

"Oh f-f-f...," he stammered and his thighs trembled as her cheek bushing gently against his inner thigh. She hungrily swallowed the nine inches he presented her and cherished every thick inch.

Jerome realized he was approaching his breaking point and quickly dislodged himself from the soothing warmth of Dana's mouth. He shifted his body downward and sumptuously connected his mouth with hers as he drove his shaft deep into her wet cavern. He was mindless with pleasure and she met his thrusts, bracing for impact, arching her back and griping his ass for more.

He was throbbing inside her and she knew he was coming just as she exploded and her inner wall muscles massaged his shaft.

She could feel the warm cum draining between her butt cheeks as he strained to breath in the crook of her neck. *'You are so bad,'* she giggled to herself, but quickly stifled her laugh just as he abruptly moved up to look down at her.

He narrowed his eyes and suddenly frowned. "Dana?"

PART 2

Dana didn't know what to say or do. The look in his eyes reflected his confusion as to whom he had just made love to or could it even be considered making love? No, Dana had been thoroughly fucked and she wasn't going to feel bad about it.

But she stifled the satisfied giggle that wanted to burst forth from her lips.

Jerome abruptly freed himself and she gasped as his movement produced an unexpected orgasmic spasm. He quickly fixed his clothes and began to pace his athletic body in front of her, as she slowly sat up feeling a slight soreness between her legs.

"Dana!" he hissed.

She nodded sheepishly as she stood up to straighten her underwear.

Surprisingly out of respect, Jerome quickly turned away from her half-naked frame. Despite what they had just shared, she smiled feeling a bit honored by his gesture. She quickly slipped into her hideous green dress and laid the wedding dress on the bed over the stain 'they' had created.

"Denise is downstairs," Dana said quietly as he turned to face her.

Initially, he flinched at the sight of her dress, but then those cool brown eyes settled upon her face. "Why?"

She shrugged and lowered her eyes, embarrassed. "I won't tell," she promised as she moved to unlock the door.

He grabbed her arm and swung her around. His lips hungrily kissed her and Dana felt her pulse quicken as he pulled her against his expansive chest, his large arms encircling her waist and his hands cupping her perfectly round bottom. Damn, he smelled good, he kissed good and he *felt* good all over.

When he moved away, he whispered, "I want you."

Breathlessly, she said sarcastically, "That sounds personal."

Shrieks and screams were coming up the stairwell and they knew Denise was coming back. Jerome practically dragged her into the closet and closed the pine louver doors just as the bedroom door swung open. Dana stood like a mannequin with her back against his chest as they faced the doors. They squinted through the wooden slats as Denise and her entourage sauntered into the room.

Denise snatched up the dress. "Hurry up!" she screamed at them.

Dana felt Jerome press his body closer to hers, but she knew he was just vying for a better view. Still his breath could be felt on the corners of her ear. She closed her eyes briefly to appreciate the close proximity of his body to hers.

Damn, all the other times in Denise's presence, Dana had admired Jerome from afar. He had never come this close unless it was a brief handshake or in passing. Never *this* close.

The sorority sisters hastily dressed Denise in her wedding gown for the second time that day.

Denise's best friend, Gloria, walked over to the disheveled bed and starred at the bedspread.

"Who messed up the bed?" Gloria asked.

Dana gasped and Jerome quickly put a hand over her mouth.

Denise stopped and looked at the bed. "Who the fuck's been flopping on my bed?"

Immediately, the women began denying having had any contact with the beautiful king sized sleigh bed that looked a hot mess.

Dana wanted to whimper in dismay, but with Jerome covering her mouth and his body pressed so damned close to hers, she was more than aware that making any sound was not an option.

"Where's Dana?" Gloria asked suspiciously.

"Who cares," Denise sneered.

"I'm asking because she's probably the one who did it."

Denise seethed, "That selfish trifling heifer. What the hell was she doing on it? Wrestling with the covers?"

Dana wanted to defend her character against Denise's crude comment but Jerome didn't seem fazed by the malevolence in his fiancée's voice. Instead, his free hand was now easing down her waist and slowly hiking up her dress. She tried to stop his hand, but then his lips began to attack the curvature of her neck.

Once her thighs were exposed, he moved his hand between her legs and pleasingly massaged her clit until her hips grinded against his groin. He had become erect, but his intentions for arousing her were different this time.

The hand that covered her mouth moved away to caress her neck and move to the front of her dress to gently squeeze her breasts, making her nipples instantly hard.

Jerome dropped to his knees and positioned her until she was pressed against the wall next to the door. The shrieks and noises on the other side of the door seem to fade away as his mouth moved in to taste her. He parted her thighs and dipped his face into her crack. His tongue sumptuously teased her puckered hole as his thick fingers dipped into her wetness heightening her excitement.

She was mindless to anything but the exhilaration he was providing in her. The tip of his delicious tongue licked her backside, down the crack and around her labia. Like a starving man, he was eating her pussy like it was his last meal and Dana was savoring every scrumptious lick.

When he stood abruptly, she felt his shaft press against her backside and with all the moistness; he easily slipped the tip of his hardened penis into her ass. A first for Dana, she instinctively tightened up, but his well-placed kisses on her neck and back instantly allowed her to relax.

His hand continued to stimulate her clit, while he pressed himself fully inside her. She bit her lip to stifle the giggle as he whispered curses of pleasure. The more his hand moved the more stimulated she became and his gyrated hips pleasurably thrusting his staff into her tightness. He had begun to sweat. She turned her head to enjoy his mouth, tasting her essence on his lips, and entwining her tongue with his.

His fingers titillated her to orgasm at the same time he exploded deep in her ass. She was soundly filled and prayed they had not made enough noise over Denise's shrieking to be heard.

"You don't taste like cow."

She had to cover her mouth to smother a giggle.

"We're so fucking bad," Jerome whispered in her ear with a deep chuckle.

In her mind, she said, *'Yes, we are. Would it be wrong to ask for more?'*

When he dislodged, she faced him and watched as he yanked a shirt off the hook to clean himself before straightening up his clothes.

He leaned in and kissed her softly. She responded tenderly, touched by his gentleness.

Taking a deep breath, he said, "I'm not marrying your sister, Dana."

Part 3

Before she could even respond, he covered her mouth as someone's voice approached to the closet. Jerome and Dana tried to move toward the back of the closet away from view.

"It's on the inside of the door," Gloria was instructing someone.

The door suddenly swung opened and a slender arm reached in, grabbed the white shawl hanging on the door and the door slammed back.

She pushed Jerome aside, quickly slipped on her dress and he hurried to zipped it up.

"Did you see that?" Gloria inquired, from the bedroom.

"What?" Denise asked.

"In the closet."

Dana shoved Jerome to the back of the closet behind the clothes and stepped in front of the door just as it swung open.

The entourage stood behind Denise, who was glaring at Dana.

"What the hell are you doing in my closet?" Denise demanded.

"And what's wrong with your hair?" Gloria instigated.

Dana snorted obviously. "I fell asleep on your bed waiting for this boring wedding to start and I messed up my hair. When I heard you all coming back I knew you'd pitch a bitch, Denise, so I ran to the closet. I was going to fix myself after everyone left" She felt as if her dark brown shoulder length tresses were laying haphazardly about her head and she began self-consciously pulling them in various directions.

A knock on the door and their mother peaked her head in. "The groom's limousine just arrived."

Denise forgot about Dana and quickly demanded someone help her with her dress and veil.

Dana stepped out the closet and closed the door, wondering how was she going to help get Jerome to the alter without Denise or her stupid soros seeing him.

"Trisha," Gloria called to one of the soros. "Go make sure the groom's men stay outside, except for Andre and we'll finish dressing Denise in the family room."

Her sister didn't protest once her dress was zipped up and her entourage followed her out the room to take the backstairs to the family room.

Gloria caught Trisha's arm and said, "Bring Andre up here. I'll stay here and make some sense out of Dana's hair." Her tone was filled with disgust as if she dreaded the deed of even touching Dana.

Dana tried to leave out, but Gloria blocked her path.

"I was going to the bathroom downstairs," Dana said. "I think I can fix my own hair."

"No, you can't and I won't have Denise's wedding ruined by you. You of all people know she's been waiting for this her whole life." Gloria moved behind Dana and feverishly worked her hair back into the ugly bun.

There was a knock on the door and Andre, Jerome's best friend and Gloria's husband, entered the room.

After a quick affectionate kiss, Gloria asked, "And how late did the groom stay out drinking?"

Andre shrugged. "Hell if I know, but while we were around him, he never touched a drop. He ducked out the hotel about four this morning, moping about how Denise's been denying him for the past six months." His tone sounded just a little bit too proud. "I thought for sure he'd sneak over here to get a piece. He hit my cell phone at eight this morning to let me know he picked up a new tuxedo, instead of coming back to the hotel to get his. I brought his anyway, just in case."

"We haven't seen him," Gloria said, finishing up Dana's hair.

"Let me call his cell," Andre said worriedly.

Dana gasped knowing if Jerome's cell rang, they would be busted like twenty-year old sneaks.

"WAIT!" Dana shouted, holding on to Andre's hand before he could press any buttons. "Shouldn't you just check the rest of the house before CALLING JEROME'S CELL PHONE TO FIND HIM?"

"You're talking crazy!" Andre snipped and wrangled his arm back before pressing the buttons on his phone.

Dana breathed a sigh of relief when seconds passed and nothing was heard.

"It went to voicemail," Andre said. "I'll call again in a minute. How's Denise? She okay? She hasn't backed out yet?" He looked really concerned.

"Bossy and snappish as usual. Let me walk you out, so you can give me some downers to calm her ass down," Gloria said, but looked back at Dana sharply. "Don't get messed up anymore before the ceremony."

Dana only nodded, all too happy to see them leave. When the coast was clear, Jerome came out the closet looking a bit sheepish, yet still devilishly handsome.

He started for her, but she put her hands out to stop him.

"Not another step, Jerome Alexander Lott," she ordered. This had been the most she had ever spoken to him or any guy. "You would be a fool to alter a very important life decision, because of a silly fling you had with your soon to be sister-in-law! Denise and I may not get along, but I refuse to be the cause of ruining the day she's waited for her entire life."

Jerome almost looked upset. "You're right."

"Furthermore, I apologize for everything. I was wrong to allow you to do that and even more wrong for letting it happen again."

He frowned.

"Aren't you going to apologize too?" she asked.

"Why? I'm not sorry."

She rolled her eyes heavenwards; overwhelmed that he could be this callous. "Then know this, Jerome. It won't happen again."

A smirk crossed those gorgeous thick lips of his making her heart jump. He approached her, was careful not to violate her personal space. "We'll see about that, Dana."

When he was gone out the room, she breathed a sigh of relief. She just needed this whole day to end. Going into the master bathroom, she quickly showered without messing up her hair. After using Denise's vanity mirror to reapply her makeup, she also borrowed a pair of her sister's underwear.

Maybe she would meet one of Jerome's nice fraternity brothers today and live happily ever after, she hoped.

Just as she was about to leave out, her sister came back into the bedroom alone.

"I was just heading downstairs," Dana said reluctantly, noting her minions were nowhere around.

"You aren't going anywhere, Dana," Denise barked, locking the door and pushing Dana toward the bed. "We've got to talk now!"

"About what?" Denise asked shocked and confused.

Putting her hands on her hips, Denise sneered angrily, "Don't think I don't know about you and Jerome!"

Part 4

Flustered and ready to pass out, Dana spoke cautiously. "I-I don't know what you mean?"

"Lying floozy!" Denise screamed, shoving her sister on the bed and standing over her. "Seven years ago, junior prom season. I was on punishment for sneaking out and you were out losing your virginity."

Dana had almost forgotten about that night. Standing up, she turned away to shed her relief. "I-Is that why you've often asked about how I lost it?"

Denise sat on the bed dejectedly. "Jerome was drunk one night about a year ago. And he was talking about the early days. How he saw me in high school. You know he use to play for Redford."

"Really?" Of course, Dana knew, but she was not about to reveal anything. She had gone to every one of the games and watched him play. She had always admired him from afar. Very far, but she never let anyone know.

"He said he saw me cheerleading for Cody High and he thought I was the prettiest girl he'd ever seen and the only reason he transferred from Florida to Michigan State University on a scholarship was because I was going there. But the real reason he said he wanted to be with me and marry me was because I was the first girl whose virginity he took in eleventh grade at River Rouge Park."

Dana slumped next to her sister devastated her stalking secret was partially out. "Did you tell him the truth?"

"I didn't dispute it," Denise admitted.

"Why?"

"Cause he's Jerome Lott. Do you know how good I look to my sorority sisters with him on my arm?" she said it so obviously.

"Yes, Denise, I do realize that and I also realize you're really shallow."

"Are you going to tell me what happened?" Denise demanded to know.

Dana sighed tiredly. She had never told anyone of that night. She had been following Jerome that day and was sitting in Rouge Park watching him at a nearby house, but she twisted the remainder of the story.

"I fell asleep on the bus and ended up at Rouge Park. The driver kicked me off at the end of the line in the park and told me to wait for the next bus. Jerome happened to be somewhere over there at this party, wandered over to me and started talking to me. He was slightly buzzed and he thought I was you." She relayed the truth from this point.

"He asked me to come into the park with him. Next thing I knew we were on the ground kissing and…well, it happened. Trust me, I was madder at myself than anything. So when I saw the next bus coming, I ran for it and jumped on. He was too busy putting on his pants, otherwise he would have caught me. A few days later he came by the house looking for you again while you were in New York for the cheerleading championship with Mom. He thought he'd really hurt me. I told him I never wanted to be reminded of that experience again and if he ever spoke of it to anyone or even me, I would never want to see or speak to him again. I guess he kept his word at least for a while."

Denise stood up looking very upset.

Yet, Dana made an observation. "Wasn't it about a year ago when he asked you to marry him?"

"Yes. He asked me that night after he said being with me in the park was a night he'd never forget! The night he had decided that I would be the woman he wanted to be with for the rest of his life."

The words stunned Dana. She just thought Jerome had been so intoxicated that he had forgotten about it since he had never mentioned it.

"So did you realize then it had been me?" Dana asked.

"Yes, Dana."

Dana stood up and faced her sister looking appalled "And you still accepted his proposal?"

"Hell yes. He's Jerome Lott. Second-round-draft-pick."

Dana stood up. "But he thinks the woman he slept with was you. Why are you deceiving him?"

"Me? You could have easily said something when I brought him home from college, Dana."

Denise was right. "I saw the big fat promise ring on your finger, Denise, and ...I guess I loved you too much to ruin how happy you seemed to be. Ever since we were little you always talked about finding a rich, handsome man, letting him buy you a big house and getting married in the huge backyard."

She could see Denise reliving their childhood dreams. That had been back in the day before the jealousy had set in, when they were more than sisters, they had been friends.

"I remember you saying it first, Dana. You always knew what you wanted. I just copied or envied it back then," Denise honestly admitted.

"So now that you know the real truth, what are you going to do?" Dana asked.

"Give you the chance to live your dreams, Dana. I'm going to give you the opportunity to marry a rich handsome man in a big backyard."

Frowning confused, Dana questioned, "What are you talking about?"

A coldness swept over Denise as if a dark curtain was being drawn in the room. "You're going to take my place and marry Jerome Lott."

Part 5

Dana touched her thick coiffed hair as if someone had just hit her on the back of the head. "What?

Denise moved behind Dana and unzipped the ugly green dress and then came around and stood in front of her.

"Unzip me, Dana. We don't have much time," Denise ordered.

Dana did as she was told, but she was confused as Denise kicked off her satin and pearl shoes and removed her veil.

"Wait, Denise!" Dana said when her sister started to put the veil on her head. "I can't take your place."

"Why not?!" Denise asked. "You and I look exactly alike."

"He'll know the difference. He's been with you for the past five years."

"Technically four and a half," Denise corrected. "But the majority of the time I was able to blow off sex. At first I said I had my morals and then there's always a period or headache to fall back on. When we were in college, school got in the way and now, he's on the road half the year and doesn't have sex during the season."

"Still, he'll know."

"You're just standing in for me during the ceremony. I can't marry him."

Dana stepped away from Denise to prevent her sister from affixing the veil to her head. "Why not?"

"Because ever since I found out my sister snuffed my man in high school, I found myself indifferent to him instantly. Besides, I love someone else," Denise stepped forward.

Dana stepped back. "Who?!"

"It doesn't matter."

"Why don't you just break it off with Jerome?" Dana asked, trying to come up with some way to find the courage to get out of that room. This was insane! Her sister had past the point of logic. Denise was on a half hour past crazy.

"I will eventually, but I can't right now. The Lions have a chance to get into the playoffs with Jerome playing this year. He'd be a hot mess if I broke it off. I would ruin his chances of signing on with another team and getting a lot more money."

"You're a crazy greedy bitch, Denise. This is morally wrong." Dana sat on the bed reconciled.

"Don't get a conscious now. You've impersonated me before, it's just this time you aren't doing it behind my back." Denise quickly did Dana's hair and then started fixing her own. "Plus, you owe me! You snuffed my man. I'd never have continued dating him if I'd known and by the time he asked me, I was given so many boons by my sorority sisters, just by association with Jerome, and I just couldn't say no." She made it sound like it was just the most inevitable thing to do.

Dana let her sister attach the veil to her head. Over and over her brain screamed, "This is crazy! He'll know."

"All you have to do is walk down the aisle, smile pretty at him, say 'I do', and walk down the aisle to all the well wishers. I'll slip away to meet you all at the reception where we'll change up and that's it."

Denise put on the ugly green dress and slipped back on her white shoes. Handing the wedding dress to Dana, she said,

"In a year or so, after the playoffs and his new contract is set in stone, I'll tell him that I have to leave him and I'll handle the divorce proceedings. He'll be so emotionally devastated he'll sign anything I put in front of him, give me the house, a nice fat monthly check and that will be that." Denise always had a way of making all things evil sound right as rain.

"And me? What about me?"

"If you keep your lips sealed, I'll write you a check for ten thousand dollars. It's all in my checking account that I've saved since college," Denise promised.

Dana could think of a million things she could do with that kind of money for her business.

Slipping on the dress, Dana took a deep breath as her sister zipped her up, handed her the beautiful bouquet of white roses, and a hug.

Dana snatched the bouquet and let the veil fall delicately over her face. She was going to do it. She was going to marry Jerome Lott.

Part 6

As soon as Dana stepped downstairs, the entourage appeared behind her and followed her into the family room. She thought it was rather hilarious to watch grown women follow her around like little puppies, waiting on her hand and foot.

"Let me touch up your make up."

"Let me bring you something to drink."

"I'll massage your hands and temples to relax you."

"You need me to hold your flowers so your arms don't get tired?"

Dana couldn't believe how they all wanted to please her. How could Denise get use to this shit? For Dana, it was just down right annoying.

"It's time," her mother said quietly, peeking her head in and then leaving, oblivious to what her daughters had done.

Jerome's father, Artie Lott, was walking the bride down the aisle. Dana and Denise's father had been MIA since they were six, so Artie didn't mind.

As she stepped out into the backyard, cameras flashed everywhere and some media swarmed around shooting her from every angle.

Dana's heart was pounding as she looked at the end of the aisle. Jerome had changed into a different tuxedo and he was as handsome as ever.

Her chest felt constricted and she was positive her stomach was going to just drop to the floor at any second. Her vision had started to blur and her legs were beginning to feel like gelatin. Artie had to nudge her and people in the crowd chuckled at her frozen state. She was practically using Artie as a clutch.

When she finally arrived next to Jerome, she could tell he had just taken a shower, and his natural smell was arousing. She couldn't stop looking at him. He looked truly happy – truly happy to stand beside her. Her mind was rewinding the morning's events. Just short of an hour, wasn't she convincing him to marry her sister? So why was he looking like that? Like he hadn't just fucked the shit out of his soon to be sister-in-law!

Still, Dana let the moment take her as he spoke his words in his smooth deep timbre voice. There was a true passion to this man and whether he was faking or not, it felt so good to hear him pledge his undying love and devotion, despite the occasionally mention of Denise's name, instead of her own.

When it was Dana's turn to speak the words to bind him to her, the words seem to flow freely from her lips, until she stumbled a bit and said her real middle name instead of Denise's. No one seemed to notice, but she quickly corrected with a glance to Denise, who didn't look at all pleased. Their mother laughed it off nervously as well, but that was it. It didn't even faze Jerome.

Once it was time for the rings, she was to go first. Denise handed her the ring and took the bouquet so Dana's hands could be free. The ring she was to give him was a heavy channel set diamond encrusted platinum ring. Its beauty momentarily spellbound her until Denise nudged her in the ribs.

After she slipped it on his thick ring finger, Andre handed Jerome a black velvet box. Jerome opened the box for her to see first. Denise pressed so tightly against her back to see it, Dana almost fell forward. Dana gasped at the blinding sight of the flawless two caret princess cut surrounded by a vintage 4-prong setting of forty half-caret diamonds.

Jerome slipped it over her finger and before the minister gave his permission, he was kissing her with his delicious thick lips.

Dana forgot everything as Jerome's thick tongue entangled with hers and sucked her essence as if she were the fountain of life.

He broke the kiss abruptly, but the look in his eyes promised of more later. Dana really wished she could be a part of what was to come for tonight and she was starting to hate Denise because she just didn't know how lucky she was to have a man like Jerome Lott. The kiss left her breathless and her body wanting, but Dana's heart was crushed.

Sadly, he really hadn't noticed the difference.

The well wishing only went on for a short while. Denise carefully diverted her sorority sisters and mother away and Gloria even helped out. Dana was positive Gloria knew what was going on. The formal reception was at a hall in Detroit, which meant Dana would have to suffer through a thirty-minute limousine ride with her new 'husband.'

Before she was dragged into the limousine, Dana was able to snatch up her purse as Denise cornered her to let her know that she would make sure her Malibu was driven to the reception hall for Dana to drive home.

Alone in the limousine Dana allowed Jerome to hold her close.

"We did it, Mrs. Lott," he said very satisfied, lightly caressing her ass. "I'm going to do my damndest to make you the happiest woman in the world."

"Didn't you just do that?" she asked sarcastically, looking straight up in his face hoping he'd see the difference.

He thought she wanted to be kissed and this he did quite well.

Dana forgot about her anger with him and allowed herself to get cozy with Jerome as he took delight in giving her a zillion kisses on her mouth, face, ears, and neck. His hands gently caressed her face and shoulders. Magically her dress disappeared and his mouth moved down to push her corset away and taste her flesh.

'*Delicious, truly delicious*,' she mused, luxuriating in his oral ministrations to each nipple as she opened his shirt. She bravely kissed his head and sucked an earlobe as he steered her to straddle his hips.

Dana didn't care that they had already made love twice earlier and he didn't seem at all tired. He kissed her as if it were the first time; he touched her as if his hands couldn't get enough and his body responded as if he hadn't made love in years.

Jesus! He was insatiable as he ripped her underwear off and opened his pants to reveal his steel root. Gripping him firmly, she pressed his tip into her. Dana grinded her hips, nibbling his lips and neck. He closed his eyes and enjoyed her gyrations as she plunged his member deeper and deeper, squeezing her inner muscles repeatedly grasping and releasing him until her intimate bliss began to literally vibrate against him.

He held her close and steered her hips to release his juices deep into hers. His hands tightly gripped her ass reveling in the orgasm she had brought them to.

"Fuck!" he cursed. "Gawd! I love you, D."

She wanted to really feel those words, but as she rested her head against his chest, she knew he would never mean them for her- not Dana. Closing her eyes, Dana fought the urge to cry because she realized after all these years, she loved Jerome Lott, her sister's husband.

Part 7

Dammit! Had she dozed off? How long had she been asleep?

Sitting up, she realized the wedding dress was laying over her like a blanket and she was sprawled over the limousine seat. Jerome was not inside the compartment and the driver was standing outside taking a long drag on a cigarette.

The vehicle was stopped in front of a municipal building. She quickly put on the wedding dress and found her lime green shoes before getting out.

Jerome was just coming out the building with a manila envelope. Once he saw her, he hurried toward her and kissed her deeply. "You look beautiful. Did you get enough rest?" he asked concerned.

"Where are we, Jerome?" she demanded to know.

"You're going to make me ruin my surprise. Can you please indulge me?"

The persuasive brown eyes captured her pulse and she couldn't deny a thing this man wanted. When they were sitting back in the limousine and it was on its way somewhere else, he said, "Did you know you snore, D? I never noticed until now. Maybe cause you usually kick me out before I'm done."

Gasping embarrassed, she said, "Only when I'm really exhausted."

He gently pushed a cowlick out her face. "It's music to my ears."

Dana couldn't help but blush as he stole yet another kiss from her.

When the limousine stopped, the driver opened the door for them and Jerome helped her out. In front of them was a quaint white towered Victorian-styled home. An older man was standing on the porch and looked happy to see them.

"I'm not taking another step until you tell me what's going on and why we aren't at the reception," she demanded.

"D, remember we talked about this? The ceremony was only for show. You forgot to get our papers in on time. Remember?"

Dana tried to look like she did, but she had no idea what he was talking about.

"Do you have the document?" the older man asked.

"Yes," Jerome said, handing the man the manila envelope. "Give us a moment, Sir."

When they were alone, she insisted to know, "Jerome, explain this to me one more time. I think I lost a few brain cells while I was snoring."

"You forgot to get our paperwork to the city clerk's office, so we paid a guy to initiate the public ceremony in Michigan just for show and I told you I would handle the private legal ceremony later. You went to get your birth certificate and mailed it down here just two days ago to a judge friend of mine, so they could have our paperwork all ready."

"Where are we?!" she exclaimed.

"Toledo," he said obviously as if she should know. "We're getting married legally, D."

Part 8

Dana wanted to scream and pass out at the same time.

Jerome caught her as her legs gave way and effortlessly helped her up the stairs. He wasn't one bit of tired and the man had initiated sex three times in one day. What the hell was he on? Stamina, her ass. He didn't look the least bit tired and he was just too nice to her.

"Are you okay, D?" he asked, concerned.

"S-Stop calling me that!" she insisted. "I-I just need to freshen up." Her breathing had become difficult and she was panting as if she were having an asthma attack.

He helped her to the door of the women's restroom inside the building and waited for her.

Dana found her cell phone in the bottom of her purse. She could barely remember, much less dial, Denise's cell phone. It had never occurred to her to put Denise's phone number in speed dial, because they had really never been close as adults. Her clients were embedded in her phone, not people from her family.

Dana knew there was something wrong with that. Her clients were closer to her than her own family, but her family really never cared about whether she lived or died. Her mother had always held Denise in high regard. Dana had never asked her mother why she played favorites to her twin daughters because Dana had always had an independent, yet docile soul.

If she knew, would it have elevated her mother to a one touch dialing status?

As soon as she heard Denise's voice, she hissed, "Where are you?"

"Shouldn't I be asking you that?" Denise asked.

There was music in the background.

"I'm freaking out in Toledo, Ohio, where *your* husband has decided to legally tie the knot on the fly, since you *obviously* failed to submit your paperwork on time. Did you hear me, Denise? I said legally! How dare you do this to me?!" She was furiously pacing between the sink and commode.

"Oh shit."

"Oh shit, what? You know something?"

"Oh shit," Denise repeated. "I don't believe he did this."

"What is he doing? What is going on, Denise? You know something I don't know."

"Oh shit."

Angrily, Dana spat, "Quit saying that!"

Denise huffed and she could hear her sister breathing heavily. "Can you leave? Can you get out of there?"

"How, Denise? We drove the limo down here. I'm in a bathroom and guess what?! He's outside waiting for me."

A knock on the door assured her that he was still out there. "D, are you okay?"

In her most pleasant voice, trying to sound happy, she said, "I'm great, Jerome. I'll be out in a moment." Getting back on the phone after turning on the water facet to cover her voice, she whispered,

"What the hell is going on, Denise? What the hell have you gotten me in?"

"Okay, listen closely, Dana. I thought I could get the wedding postponed about a week ago when I admitted to Jerome that I hadn't gotten my birth certificate and turned in our papers in Michigan in enough time to get married. He refused to listen and said that we'd just do the ceremony for show and then go down to Toledo later on a run."

"A run?"

"You know, a Toledo run. Where you can get married in like twenty-four hours? He'd invited the whole NFL and some really big celebrities to the ceremony we had today, so I just figured, hey, what the hell, we wouldn't go down till afterwards and I'd just stall until later."

"So why the hell did I have to participate in the ceremony this morning, Denise?"

"I told you, Dana, I'm in love with someone else, and he couldn't bare me walking down that aisle to Jerome."

"He was at the wedding?"

"Yes, Dana!" Denise said exasperated. "He told me if I walked down that aisle, he'd tell Jerome the truth, so I had to do this. I had to use you. I don't want to lose him."

"And you don't want to lose Jerome, *either*," Dana said confused and frustrated. "This is some fucked up shit, Denise. You're having your cake and eating it too."

"You owe me!"

"Enough with the owing, Denise. What the hell am I doing in Toledo with your supposed husband?"

"Like I said, Dana, I thought this would take place later. Jerome's always an 'I'll-do-it-later' man. Always." Denise huffed.

"I could just call you in about five minutes when you're probably at the alter and say there's some kind of family emergency."

"That would work," Dana agreed, calming down a little. "Do ten minutes and don't be late."

Denise promised. "And I'm sorry for all this mess, Dana. When you get back here, we'll figure everything out."

Dana washed her face and applied some lipstick and gloss. Turning off the water, she took a deep breath and stared at her deep cinnamon eyes and her flushed caramel smooth complexion. This couldn't really be happening to her.

Tucking the phone in her bra to keep it close, she opened the door to the bathroom to find Jerome sitting by the door, looking a bit worried.

Jerome stood as she stepped out. He had the veil from the car draped over his wrist. Standing before him like this, away from the crowd at the ceremony where they were all alone, she felt drawn to remember that first night they were together. He seemed so enchanted by her and he kept telling her how he thought she was the prettiest girl he'd ever seen.

'I feel like I've waited my whole life for you, D,' he said that night before she allowed him to lean down and kiss her softly and then take her under a big oak tree in the park.

He kissed her right now, in the present and it still felt like they were under the big oak tree, hidden by the traffic, in the dim evening of a Detroit summer.

"I know what you're thinking," Jerome said, lightly playing his fingertips over her cheek.

"What?" she asked.

"Our first time."

She blushed as he took her hand and kissed her inner wrist.

"I always think of that night, D," he admitted.

The older man stood in the doorway and cleared his throat. Neither had heard him come in.

"It's time, Mr. Lott. Are there rings for this ceremony? I'd like to look over them before I bless them."

Jerome still had her hand clutched and looked down at their rings. "Yes, we have our rings." He removed his.

Dana patted her chest nervously where she had jammed her cell phone.

He held her hand and tried to gently remove her ring, but it wouldn't budge. She tried as well, but it seemed pretty much lodged in place.

"Let me try again," he said, gently getting her finger, extending it and wrapping those thick lips around the base of it, while his tongue massaged her skin.

They never broke eye contact and she found herself becoming aroused yet again. Damn, her attraction for him. Damn, what this sexy ass man could do to her libido!

The ring eventually slipped off, as they began to forget their purpose for being here.

The older man had to clear his throat again and Jerome guided her into a chapel, near the back of the house.

As they stood in front of the alter, Jerome took her veil and moved in close to help her put it on. Again his gentleness amazed her.

"You're so big," she noted out loud, not meaning to.

He frowned. "I'm only three hundred, D. There are other guys on the team bigger than me."

"I mean, you seem bigger from this morning."

Looking seriously at her, he said, "I didn't see you this morning."

Catching her mistake, she said obviously, "Yes, you did. The ceremony, silly."

He relaxed a little.

"That was only a couple of hours ago and our ceremony started at eleven. That's considered afternoon." He adjusted her veil once more and moved it over her face. "This time I want to see your face. I think this idea was perfect, D."

Annoyed at the reminder that they were standing in front of an alter and her phone had yet to ring, she thought she could pick an argument with him. "Why do you just call me, Dee and not my whole name?"

A secret smile graced his lips. "I've called you, D since the day I've met you. Don't you remember?"

She remembered now and whatever argument she was going to pick left her thoughts.

There was a clock behind the old man's head, and all she could do was watch it. She couldn't even be bothered with the preparation the old man and Jerome spoke about.

"I'm a big fan of your skills, Mr. Lott," the old man said. "I watch your games all the time. I never miss one."

Jerome smiled proudly. He almost looked as happy as he looked after a great orgasm. Denise was right. To crush him now would probably devastate his career.

"There's only one more paper you have to sign and we can began the ceremony, Mr. Lott." The old man placed a form on the table in front of them.

Three people came in the room and helped the old man prepare for the ceremony. All the while, the three people seemed to be more focused on Jerome than on Dana. She didn't mind that no one paid her attention because she was on the brink of having an uncontrollable panic attack.

Dana took a quick look at the paper and gasped. Her name was on the paper. Not Denise's. Her sister had turned in Dana's birth certificate. Not her own. Did she think Jerome wouldn't see this? Denise had been preparing to dupe Jerome the whole time. The plan to use Dana in her place must have come later before Denise thought of the plan to use Dana's name to falsify the wedding. Damn Denise!

"Usually I have the papers signed afterwards," the old man stated, "But while you're putting your John Hancock down, Mr. Lott, I thought you wouldn't mind signing some other things for an autograph too, 'cause I know you'd be too busy later with this pretty lady." He handed Jerome the pen first and Dana just wanted to scream.

'Ring phone, ring!'

Jerome quickly signed the paper, not even looking it over, and then turned and autographed some paraphernalia for the old man. Two of the witnesses brought items for Jerome to sign as well, while the old man turned to her.

"I do need to verify your identification, ma'am," the older man said.

Dana hurriedly jammed her hand in her purse and found her ID. The old man took more than a moment to look at it and then handed her the pen just as Jerome was about to look over her shoulder at the paper.

She scribbled her name and handed the old man the paper and the pen before Jerome could see whose name she was writing.

The old man looked at the signature and then handed her back her identification, which she promptly shoved into her purse. Looking at the clock, she noted it had been nine minutes since the phone conversation.

Jerome took her hand and the old man began to speak the words that would bind them to her.

"Do you, Jerome Lott, take BEEP-BEEP-BEEP as your lawfully married wife?"

The phone had rung and Dana almost screamed in joy.

BEEP, BEEP, BEEP

"I do," Jerome said sincerely.

"And do you BEEP BEEP BEEP take Jerome Lott to be your lawfully wedded husband?"

She dug the phone out her bra and looked down at the display. It was Denise's phone.

"It's my sister," she told Jerome and put the phone to her ear, "Hello...Umm..Dana?"

There was no answer. The line had gone dead and she was just left with nothing on the other end.

Jerome took the phone and put it in his pocket. Dana started to protest, and he said, "If it's important, she'll call back. I'm sure she's just worried about you not being at the reception, but she'll understand once we get back, Love. You can call and explain everything."

Dana didn't know how to respond and the phone was not ringing, no matter how much her subconscious willed it. If she finished this ceremony there was going to be a whole lot of explaining to do!

"Please finish," Jerome told the older man.

"We're just waiting for her," the old man said.

"Waiting for what?" Dana snapped annoyed as seconds passed and there was no phone ringing.

Jerome tightened the grip on her hand and edge closer. "D, we're waiting for you to answer the question."

Dana's breath was caught in her throat as she stared up in Jerome's eyes. She just had to stall for time. Playing dumb, she asked, "W-What question?"

Her sister's supposed-to-be husband didn't seem the least annoyed or upset as he chuckled a bit and calmly asked, "Do you want to marry me?"

Part 9

In the back of Dana's head, she could hear Denise's voice repeating, *'We don't want to hurt him. We don't want to hurt him.'*

"Do you or don't you, girl?" One of the witnesses impatiently asked.

Jerome put a hand up to hush the onlookers and leaned toward her ear. "I love you, D."

She whispered back as tears welled up in her eyes. "I know."

"And I'm going to give you the world and protect you from everything bad."

"I know." The tears were now running down her face. This magnificent man was too good for her sister.

"From this day forward, it'll just be you and me. No one else. From this time forward, we'll make each other happy. I can't live without you." Wrapping those burly arms around her small waist, he pulled her body tightly against his. Though her head only came to his chest, he curved his body so his head was still on the side of her face.

How she had always wanted to hear a man say those wonderful words to her and hold her close like this forever.

Kissing her neck and cheek in a sweet caress, he said, "Marry me, D. Say I do, please."

"I do."

Again he didn't wait for permission to salute her. And Dana responded with just as much passion despite how her heart was feeling. Lawd, the man was irresistible. How could Denise not be in love with him?

They barely got the rings back on before he was sweeping her up, carrying her out the chapel and up some stairs.

"Where are we going?" Dana questioned.

"Our suite. This is a hotel too." He quickly kissed her, effortlessly continuing to carry her down a long hallway and up another set of stairs until they came to some double doors.

Jerome didn't put her down until they were inside of the room.

"Shouldn't we get back to the reception, Mr. Lott?" she asked, trying not to sound agitated.

"Everyone, except your sister and mother, knew we weren't going to be there for the party. I'm sure Gloria and Andre will let them know so they won't worry. That reception was really just for the public and to raise some money for my youth athletic foundation. Remember, Mrs. Lott?"

She pretended that she did and smiled liking the fact that he called her that.

"I'll go get our bags out the car, while you get showered and changed. I know you're tired." Gently pecking her cheek, he caressed her lips and chin forcing her to look up into his beautiful brown eyes. "Marrying you today was the best thing in my life, D."

"Ditto."

"Say it," he ordered.

Looking confused, she asked, "What?"

"You know what I want to hear."

'No, I don't, cause I'm not who you think I am,' her thoughts screamed. "Refresh my memory, Jerome, please."

"Say you love me. You know I love to hear it from your lips."

Dana thought that was so simple from a man who looked so complicated. "I love you, Jerome Alexander Lott."

A bright smile graced those lips and all his teeth showed. "Do you really, D?"

It felt so good to say, "Yes, I do." Lying about her feelings for him came too easily. *Maybe because your feelings are close to the truth?'* she asked herself.

Jerome was about to leave to go get the bags, but when she called his name, he instantly stopped at the door.

"Can I have my phone back? I want to make sure my mother's okay and not worried about me."

"Sure," he said, handing her the phone.

When he was gone, she called Denise's cell phone, but it immediately went into voicemail as if it were off. On the third try Dana left a voice message, including the number to the hotel/chapel she'd gotten from a matchbook left on the nightstand.

Just as she hung up the phone, Jerome came in the room quicker than she thought it would take to get all the bags. Had he run to the car and back with all their bags?

"You haven't started your shower yet?"

He was being nothing but nice to her and she just didn't know how to take it. How could she pretend to be Denise around him when she didn't know how Denise was around Jerome?

Obviously Denise didn't act like her true self around him, because that would mean Dana should have been bitchy and snappish all the time, which she wasn't. So, however she was acting it must have been right because Jerome hadn't said a thing.

"I'm sorry," she said.

"There's nothing to be sorry for, D. I just figured you were waiting for me to join you."

Blushing, she rolled her eyes heavenward at his playfulness. She went into the bathroom, turned on and adjusted the water to a perfect temperature.

It had been a long day and she just wanted to lie on a real bed and sleep for a while. Removing the wedding dress, she wanted to toss it in the garbage, but didn't. Instead, she laid it over a stool in the room and relieved herself.

Quickly, she got in the shower and scrubbed her body all over with the sweet smelling honey-milk soap. When stepping out the shower, she realized Jerome had come in, removed the wedding dress and replaced it with a thick robe and a black bag.

Inside were Denise's toiletries: expensive lotions, perfumes and makeup.

Things Dana usually went to the dollar store and bought, Denise have would spent no less than a hundred dollars to purchase.

Dana enjoyed the way the more expensive lotion actually moisturized her skin and how the perfumes and body butter fragrances actually clung to her body making it a sensual playground for the nose.

Exiting out the bathroom, Dana's nose was graced with the smell of delicious home cooked fried chicken, green beans, and macaroni and cheese.

"I know you hate soul food, D, but this was what they were serving downstairs. I'll go out and find something else."

She shook her head, but then remembered Denise would have expected him to. "It's our wedding night. We shouldn't be a part," she said, explaining her actions.

He looked relieved. "You eat while I take my shower and we'll lay down together."

Her brow rose wickedly at the thought of being in a bed fully naked with Jerome.

"Just sleep," he insisted reading her thoughts. "I know how you only like it once a day, D. I said I will always respect your wishes when I married you." He grabbed a guest robe and went into the bathroom.

As soon as the shower started, she felt comfortable to run over to the table where the food was. There was an empty plate beside her full plate, which indicated that he had already eaten.

Dana had to wonder, as she gobbled down the food, what other stipulations had Denise enforced upon the man. And how much did he love Denise to bend over backwards for her? Although Jerome seemed the dominant one in the relationship, it seemed that his weakness was his love for Denise.

Instead of drinking the wine provided, she found some water in the small guest refrigerator.

Denise was the drunk. Dana hated alcohol, but she hoped Jerome wouldn't insist on drinking. There was a fully stocked bar in the room, but it didn't look as if he had removed anything.

She turned the lights low and used the matches to light the candles around the room. It was just seven in the evening and the sun had yet to set, so she drew the curtains to give the room a feel of ambience. Going through the bags, she found two CD cases in his items. They were the same design, but they had different letters on the front. She waved this off and figured it was because of what they contained. When she found a CD she liked, she put the case back and hoped he would forgive her rummaging.

When he emerged from the bathroom, she gasped. With just a towel around his wait, she realized this was truly the first time she had seen his body – all his body – and words couldn't begin to describe how astoundingly cut he was. Muscles bulged from every inch and not one centimeter of fat was on his body. Gawd, he was a black Adonis that should be admired and adored.

Dana could easily do this.

"Stop looking at me like that, D," he chuckled. "I said we were going to sleep."

He removed the towel and her eyes widened. Even flaccid his darkened shank hung at least seven good inches. Her mouth had begun to water and as he approached the bed, she timed it just right to fall to her knees and engulfed him in her mouth.

"D-Damn-" Again, he was lost for words as the tip of him pressed into the back of her throat. The velvety skin felt good on her tongue as she withdrew and then plunged right back down flickering her tongue, knowing it would drive him crazy.

"Did you pick up some tips from your bridal shower, D? Cause you never-" He stopped mid-sentence as she released him and wrapped her warm orifice around his orbs. Her tongue tenderly laved the skin past the orbs near his nether and then she licked from that region all the way back to the tip of his shaft.

This time as she swallowed him, she didn't stop her oral manipulation until he was gripping her shoulders, throwing his own head back and releasing deep down her throat. Even then she continued to suck him until the spasms died down.

"You didn't have to, D," he panted as she stood up.

"I wanted to, Jerome."

He pushed the robe off her shoulders and carried her to the bed. As he cuddled behind her, he pulled her body in the nook of his own. They quietly spooned, enjoying the comfort of each other until they slipped into a peaceful slumber.

*　　*　　*　　*　　*

The most sensational feeling overcame her and she moaned in glory as her body exploded in the best orgasm she could have ever experienced in her sleep.

Opening her eyes suddenly, she looked down only to meet those wicked brown eyes. His mouth was attached to her moist aperture and his tongue and fingers were busily bringing her back to arousal. That didn't take long and soon she found herself clutching the sheets, biting her lip and moaning her pleasure.

He didn't stop and her body was drenched in sweat as she endured his oral pleasures before she passed out again.

*　　*　　*　　*　　*

When she awoke again, he was sound asleep next to her and she slid out the bed without disturbing him. Her phone was in her robe, which she snatched on the way to the bathroom to relieve her bladder and call Denise's phone.

"Hello?" a familiar deep voice answered.

"Andre?" Dana questioned. "What are you doing with Denise's phone?"

"Um...she left it...she and Gloria...well, your mother wanted to go to Neiman Marcus and she took her."

"She's with Gloria?" Dana asked. So Gloria was in on this cause Gloria wouldn't be caught dead with Dana in public.

"Um...no...isn't this Denise on the phone?" He sounded so bad at lying. "Dana left her purse at the reception and Gloria picked it up."

She hung up the phone. What the hell was going on?

Part 10

When she was with Jerome, she was his 'D.' That shy, innocent girl he had met so long ago. They could talk about anything. He could make her laugh and every endearment of love made her heart beat just a little bit faster.

He made love to her like his life depended on it and she found that she matched his passion and wantonness every time he touched her. His endurance in bed was overwhelming and amazing, but she enjoyed it so much.

They had lunch the next day at a small café not too far from the hotel/chapel and then he took her shopping at a mall all the way in Cleveland. It felt weird being able to buy whatever she wanted. He indulged her when she wanted to go into a bookstore and even read aloud to her quietly on a couch in the loft part of the bookstore.

That was until some fans of his recognized him and came over for autographs. Afterwards, they walked around Cleveland visiting the sites and then returned to the hotel/chapel to pack.

Upon their return, Jerome went into the bathroom just as the old man came to the doorway with the manila envelope Jerome had given him yesterday. "This is the official certificate for marriage."

Dana took the envelope from the man and put it in her purse and then quietly let him out before Jerome knew he'd come.

As they drove back to Detroit in the limousine, he spoke seriously with her. "You know I leave for spring training in two weeks, D."

She hadn't, but then she realized that Denise had planned it just perfectly. Since he would be gone on spring training and then the football season starting, he really wouldn't be home permanently until almost the end of the year.

"I'd love for you to come visit me on the road more, this year," he said. "You only came once last year. At the end of the year, we'll go on our honeymoon as plan."

"I'll try," she said rather elusively.

He kissed her left knuckles. "You haven't said anything about the ring."

Dana didn't know what she was supposed to say. It wasn't even hers to keep. Before she could respond, her phone rung.

Pulling it out, she almost cursed. It was one of her clients, which she knew she couldn't talk to, so she pushed it into voicemail.

Jerome looked a little annoyed, but he didn't say anything. The rest of the trip to Detroit was quiet and Dana knew there was something more going on between Jerome and Denise than what they allowed other people to know; yet Dana couldn't ask.

When they got to the house, he made a silly excuse to go into the family room, while she coordinated with the butler getting the luggage upstairs and into the master bedroom.

Opening the closet, she couldn't believe twenty-four hours ago her life had completely changed.

"Dana!" Denise hissed, popping out of nowhere in the closet frightening her.

Dana covered the scream that flew out her mouth. "You scared the bejesus out of me! Where did you come from?"

Denise moved away from the doorway and pressed the wall in the back of the closet. "When I had the house built, I had them install a secret stairway that goes to the guest quarters."

"Does Jerome know about this?" Dana asked.

"Of course not," Denise answered, confidently.

Dana turned to her sister. "What happened to you yesterday?! Why did Andre have your phone?"

Denise shrugged and walked past Dana to look in the shopping bags. "What'd he buy me?"

"Denise?!" Dana said in frustration. "What is going on? Why was my name on your marriage certificate?"

"Because I couldn't use mine," Denise said obviously. "When I went down to vital records the clerk didn't notice I was a twin and retrieved the wrong document. I didn't say anything and when Jerome came up with that plan to marry in Toledo, I thought this would be another way to stall. I was going to go along with the plan and then when we signed the papers, I'd pretend like I just realized it was your birth record and we'd have another way to stall again, but we wouldn't be able to get married legally in the time we needed since he'd be leaving for spring training."

Denise looked at the items bought in disgust.

"You have awful taste, Dana. And what the hell am I going to do with books?"

"You're changing the subject," Dana said, removing the envelope from her purse and handing it to her sister. "I'm now legally married to him. You know that right?"

Denise took the envelope. "We'll figure something out, sister. I'll talk to my lawyer tomorrow."

"D!" Jerome called, coming up the stairs.

Denise shoved Dana toward the closet. "Get the ring off and just push on the wall to go down the stairs."

Before Dana could say another thing, Denise slammed the closet door just as the master bedroom door opened. Dana didn't use the secret passage; she stayed and watched them.

"Are you done?" he asked, coming in the room.

"Yes...I mean no. Dammit Jerome, we just got here!" Denise snapped. "Why are you even bothering me? We just spent the last twenty-four hours together. Don't you have some friends to see or something?"

Jerome's face tightened in annoyance - That same annoyance that he had expressed in the car. "Where's your ring?"

Dana began to busily suck on her finger to pull the ring off.

"I must have left it in my jacket. I didn't want to bruise it while I unpacked." Denise came over to the closet as Dana moved out of view should Denise decide to open the door.

Denise only outstretched her arm and Dana dropped the ring in her sister's hand.

"See it's right here," Denise snipped. "Now go on and leave me alone."

Jerome left and Dana sighed in sorrow. He was a man torn between loving and hating the same woman, but he didn't even know there were two different women. Since meeting her, Jerome had been duped and he deserved so much better. It just wasn't fair.

Part 11

Dana followed Denise's instructions and found the guest garage where her car was parked. She drove home and returned all the phone calls from her clients for her business before going back to work.

Looking down at her empty finger, she wondered if she could ever find someone like Jerome to share her life. Just remembering the wonderful way they had gotten along and made love, made her heart long to feel that way all the time.

By the time she realized she was hungry, it was going on ten at night. She found a Hot Pocket in the back of her freezer and scarfed it down before she got ready for bed.

This was her life. Work, sleep, work some more and do the daily humdrum tasks of living. Little else. For some reason, there didn't seem to be a need for anything else until she realized how much she really loved Jerome Lott.

'Damn, Dana, stop thinking about him! You knew from the beginning he was never going to be yours.'

Her doorbell rung. She checked the time and went to the door in just her bathrobe since she was preparing to take a long hot shower to try to forget about the last twenty-four hours of her life.

Jerome stood under the porch light. He'd changed clothes, yet he was still as handsome as ever.

"What are you doing here?" she asked. Her sister's husband had never been to her home before and she was surprised that he knew where it was.

"We have to talk," he said, brushing past her.

"Please come in," she said sarcastically, closing the door. "Are you alone?"

"Yes, I've been alone all day, Dana, since we got back." He started to pace in her front room.

"You're married now, Jerome. You can't be alone. You've got a wife."

Jerome stopped pacing. "That isn't the same woman I married. Dammit, for twenty-four hours, she was different. She was like the first time. She hadn't been that way in years – hell, decades!"

Dana stepped away from him pretending nonchalance. "I think you should be talking to your wife and not me. I told you nothing like that would happen again."

"I just need someone to listen, Dana, and you're the only one I can talk to about everything. I need you to listen before I go crazy!" he stressed.

She sincerely looked at him and he did look like a man on the verge of insanity "Want some coffee? Tea?"

"Anything," he said, relieved she was willing to hear him out.

He followed her into the kitchen, and sat at a small dining room table. She could hear the cheap material squawking at the weight of him.

"I don't think I should get involved in my sister's personal life, Jerome," Dana said, voicing her complaint now as she fixed their cups, while the water boiled. "Matter-of-fact, I'm feeling damn guilty about what I did."

Snorting in disgust, he said, "Don't. Denise has been cheating on me a long time."

This news took her by surprise. "What do you mean? How long have you known and why did you marry her if you knew?"

He stood up and helped her carry the cups to the sitting area and even poured the water for her. She watched as he put in three spoonfuls of sugar and two creams; just the way she liked it.

"Is that fine?" he asked, sitting across from her.

"Perfect."

"You didn't even taste it."

She had not been talking about the coffee.

"So you were telling me about Denise?" Changing the subject was her best bet or she would be spilling secrets like a flooding river.

"I knew there was something going on since we graduated from college, but I thought once I received the pro-contract, it would be enough to make her happy."

"You'd be able to buy her monogamy. Is that what you were thinking, Jerome?"

Bashfully and ashamed, he nodded.

"I wanted to give her the world and when she gave me the opportunity to be with her again in college, I told myself I never wanted to lose her, but she wasn't the same person I had met in high school, yet..." He was lost for words.

"You loved her."

Nodding, he sipped his coffee.

"I figure sooner or later she'd come around, but sex with her was dismal, and her demands and shallowness were becoming worse and worse. When I left to go pro, she seemed glad to see me go and hateful when I returned." Sighing, he said, "I left my bachelor party early to do a lot of thinking, Dana. I convinced myself to come to the house that morning and tell Denise we were fooling ourselves and to call this whole sham off."

"But?"

He was staring down at the coffee and didn't answer.

When more seconds passed and he still didn't answer, she said, "It didn't go that way, Jerome. Remember, I was there."

Slowly his golden brown eyes met hers.

"I know. You were there. Not this stuck up shallow bitch I've been dealing with for the past four years."

Oh Gawd, did he know the truth about the first time and yesterday? Dana bit her lips, not wanting to reveal anything.

"I figured it out, Dana," Jerome announced. "I figured everything out."

She almost bit off the ceramic cup waiting for him to say something, but he wanted her to ask. He wanted her to speak, so she spoke.

"What did you figure out?"

"College changes a lot of people. Denise joined the sorority. She was away from her element and then you dropped out shortly before I transferred over there. That must have been devastating to her. You're twins. You were most likely close."

This time she wanted to snort, 'Not likely,' but didn't.

"Yet, when I walked in that room and saw who I thought was her standing there looking beautiful and the way you looked at me as if I was the best thing since slice bread, I forgot what I was going to say to her and..." Again he trailed off, almost blushing.

"And when you realized it was me?"

"I missed being adored. You, at that time, looked as if you adored me and, hell, if I had gone that far on cheating on Denise, then I might as well fulfill all my fantasies right?"

Now it was her turn to blush. She had let him go where no man had ever gone before and enjoyed every moment of it.

"But yet you still walked down that aisle with her, Jerome, and you looked as if you were in love when ...when I saw you taking your vows." She had been about to say, 'when we spent the entire weekend together.'

"Because, Dana," he said, sitting back frustrated again. "She looked at me like that as we stood there taking our vows. She was looking at me like I was the answer to her prayers. Like she loved me. Like she had been waiting for this moment her entire life." His gazed locked with Dana's. "Like you look at me now."

Part 12

Dana didn't know who advanced first, but seconds later their lips were passionately locked and she was enjoying yet again the feel of his mouth. She knew she could never get tired of his touch and she wanted nothing more than to feel his body inside her.

He pulled her chair effortlessly towards her and scooped her waist up until she was sliding onto his lap straddling his hips. Her robe opened and as one hand massaged her generous backside, the other was busy tweaking a nipple and sliding down into her wetness.

Without straining, he lifted up out of the chair and hoisted her onto the counter. Their kisses never stopped and by this time her robe was quickly sliding from her body, while his shirt and pants were opened.

A groan of pleasure escaped his lips as she caressed the front of his pants then firmly gripped his manhood from the outside of his underwear. He was hard as a rock and she knew he would easily slide inside her. Damn, he was a drug she was slowly developing an addiction for and relishing every moment of her lack of control. The more she had, the more she wanted him.

But wait…

Pushing him away suddenly, she wrested her lips reluctantly from the passionate kiss.

"No, we can't, Jerome."

His hot gaze fought the testosterone urges that were driving him, but when she repeated what she said again to him in a very firm voice, he pulled his control together right before her eyes. Moving away slightly, he looked up in her eyes. She got a real close up look of the barreled muscular chest and the dark nipples that were erect as well. Her mouth watered to nibble upon them and ignite his passion again.

"You're right," he heaved grudgingly. "We shouldn't."

"You're a married man, remember."

"Hell, people cheat on each other every day when they're married, Dana." He leaned forward.

She knew she was no match for him in strength, yet she firmly placed her hands on his shoulders to prevent him from moving forward anymore.

"But you're not that type of man. You've been faithful so far and one indiscretion won't lead you down the path to continued adultery."

He looked longingly in her eyes and amused. "Are you always so righteous, Dana?"

That he would actually find her amusing endeared her even more to him. Jerome Lott was no man. He was the perfect man in love with a woman he really wasn't in love with.

Jerome moved away, but not before helping her from the counter and then turning to give her an opportunity to close her robe, while he fixed his clothes.

"This is really pathetic, Dana," he realized as he turned around. "I'm in love with my wife, but I can't stop the feeling that I want her sister just as much."

He held Dana's left hand and fondly caressed her ring finger. The finger that had just held the fat rock he married her with just hours ago.

"Do you ever watch me play, Dana?"

"If you're trying to find out what my attraction is to you, Jerome, then just go look in the mirror. You're handsome, athletic-"

He cut her off. "I don't want just what any woman would say, Dana." Looking down at her finger as he continued to caress it, he asked, "Did you ever go to my games in high school?"

She looked down at the floor unable to look at him and lie. "No, Jerome. I wasn't a sports groupie. I was a bookworm. I went to school, came home, did an occasionally part-time job and went back to school."

"That's funny because even though Denise said she only came to cheer at the games, I always felt...I always felt someone was watching me. I'd be warming up for a game and then all of a sudden, this wave of..." He couldn't think of the words again.

"I felt her. I felt my D watching me, loving me from afar."

He touched her chin and raised her eyes to his. "Why are you crying, Dana?"

Again she had to lie. "Because someone who loved that much doesn't deserve to be hurt."

He probably thought she was talking about Denise, but in truth, she was talking about him. Yes, Dana had watched him. She had gone to every game, every after-party. She had been the wallflower, the poster child to staying out the limelight - watching and wishing for him.

Wishing she could have the big home and fancy car with him. Wishing she could lie down tonight in his arms and kiss away all his worries and stress - make him feel like a king and in return, he would make her feel like a queen.

Tenderly, he wiped the tears from her cheek and lightly brushed his lips against her.

"Yeah, you're right, Dana. You're always right, but I miss my D. I miss the way she made me feel, I missed what she did to me and I'm tired of getting her every blue moon." He sounded very bitter.

"I need more. At least when I'm with you, I feel almost like that, although I'll never get to that point again unless I'm with my D. That's just for her to have and I can't seem to stop myself from feeling that way. I'm sorry for using you, Dana. I'm wrong for that."

They hugged each other, each for different reasons.

When he left, Dana didn't bother to take a shower. She wanted to dwell in the essence of his scent, at least for tonight since forever was never promised.

'He was never going to be yours from the beginning. That's why you forced yourself to forget, Dana. That's why you convinced yourself that you could handle Denise getting married to him.'

Closing her eyes in distressed sleep, she knew she would dream of him as his scent permeated her nostrils.

*   *   *   *   *

Deep in sleep, the sound of her doorbell ringing at two in the morning awoke her. She had only slipped on a thin white nightgown, so her thoughts were consumed with the rapid knocking on her door as if the house were burning down.

Opening the door, she couldn't believe Jerome stood there again. He had changed his clothes, yet again, to the ones he had been wearing when they had arrived home from the honeymoon.

Before she could ask what he was doing there, he pressed his lips against hers and kissed her so powerfully it left her breathless.

"I thought about it and damn adultery, I want you, Dana." He swept her up, carried her in the house, kicked the door closed and conveyed her straight to her bedroom.

Dana didn't protest. For one night she was going to have the man she had dreamed of having since her childhood. The boy who had taken her virginity. Dana was going to be Dana tonight in Jerome Lott's arms and he would call out her name and love every moment of being with her.

Jerome Lott made love to her like he needed her just as much as she needed him and as they orgasmed together, he held her close.

Calming themselves an hour later, he held her in his arms and talked about his reasoning for returning to Dana.

"I went home and she told me I would have to sleep in the guest room. She blamed a headache, but damn, Dana. I'm a man. I have needs. She put me off far too long while we weren't married and I have waited like a damn fool thinking once I married her things would be different."

Sitting up, she looked down at his large body that partially filled her full-size bed.

"You came over at two in the morning because your wife denied you sex?"

"No," he said, sitting up looking dead at her despite the dimness in the room.

"I came over at two in the morning to feel again. She'd been denying me for over a year and then she becomes this insatiable woman on our wedding night, but then reverts back to this frigid bitch twenty-four hours later. I couldn't take it anymore. I had to come where I knew-"

"Don't say another word to me, Jerome," she said, cutting him off moving to get out of bed and demand his immediate departure.

He grabbed her arm and pulled her on top of him.

"Please Dana. Not you too."

Frustrated, she asked, "Do you know I'll go to hell for breaking up a marriage? I'm the other woman, Jerome."

"I needed to talk too. I mean that's why I came back. I was frustrated and I had no where to go."

"There are a million hotels out there and you can certainly the pick of the litter."

"Yeah, and a million bartenders who would love to hear my story, but I didn't want them, Dana. I wanted you. I wasn't going to touch you, but dammit, woman, you opened the door with that little thing on and you looked so damn good that I couldn't help myself."

She was confused. Very confused. At one moment she was suppose to be mad at him, but then he would go and say the sweetest thing and make her forget her anger.

"What did you want to talk about?"

"Just that and then I was going to ask to lay on your couch."

"You know the couch is still available."

He looked insulted. "You're serious, Dana?."

"Jerome, I can't stand the thought of sleeping with my sister's husband no matter how much I'm attracted to him. I feel guilty. Matter-of-fact, take the keys by the door and there's a guest room downstairs in my office."

"What if I'm not done talking?"

Folding her arms over her sheet-covered breast defensively, she asked, "What is there to speak about?"

"I'm quitting the team, Dana, and I don't know how to tell Denise."

She was startled and tried to make light of the situation. "You're talking crazy. That's kind of drastic over sleeping with your sister-in-law, Jerome."

He chuckled genuinely humored by her. "You aren't why I'm quitting the team. I've thought about this long and hard, Dana. It was way before I...well tonight."

"And what about your wedding day?" she questioned.

"What about it? My decision to leave football has nothing to do with where I lay my dick at night."

His crudeness caught her off guard, but she said nothing to the fact.

"So why are you leaving?"

"I've accomplished what I wanted to accomplish. I wanted to know if I was good enough to play pro and I am. The team doesn't know yet, and my agent thinks I'm a fool because I'm guaranteed over ten million, but I don't want to go on living like this. I need to be myself. I need to be me. I envy you, Dana."

This was a bold statement coming from such a confident man. "Why? You live in a luxurious home, you're making millions a year. I'm barely making my house and car note, I'm trying to catch up on work on old equipment and I can't expand until I can up my production, but I can't do that until I can afford to get new equipment. I should be envying you."

"You live simple. You live like you want to live. You're not trying to impress anyone. You can take one day at a time and just go from there. That's a luxury."

She really didn't want to divulge anymore of her own personal problems to him, so she got back on the subject. "And what are your plans afterwards?"

"I've got plans," he said quite confidently. "I already have investments working in my favor and on top of that I've been working on several athletic boards, speaking engagements, the youth foundation, business developments and so forth. Trust me, I will live comfortably when this is all over."

"Denise is not the kind of woman who wants to live comfortably."

"I know," he sighed as he got out of bed and began dressing.

She tried not to look upset about him going, but she was. Dammit, this was her husband, not Denise's. Why should her selfish sister have the pleasure of this man's company when in truth he really belonged to Dana?

And why was Dana keeping her mouth closed? Denise could give a fig's ass about Dana.

Still, her lips would not spill the beans. Somehow Denise did have a special place in her heart. She was her twin.

"But you play so well, Jerome, why wouldn't you want to keep doing it?' she asked.

He stared directly at her and announced, "Because I'm not Jerome Lott, Dana."

Part 13

There was a moment of silence as Dana tried to digest this information, yet there was no way of swallowing it. "What do you mean you're not Jerome Lott?"

He was finished dressing and leaned over the bed. "Have you ever been in love with two people at the same time, Dana?" He changed the subject instantly as if he hadn't made an off the wall declaration.

Now she really thought he was losing it. "No, Jerome. I've never and you're not in love with me. We just like to fuck."

That gorgeous smile appeared on his face. "I love an honest woman, Dana."

"You don't love me," she reemphasized. "You've loved Denise all your life. Remember?"

"I said that?"

"This evening at the table."

He frowned as if he hadn't meant to admit that to anyone.

Dana wanted to get back on what she was confused about. "What about you not being Jerome Lott and falling in love with two people have to do with anything?"

Jerome sat back on the bed and lightly traced her lips with his fingertips as if he was trying to remember each and every inch of her.

"Nothing, Dana. They have nothing to do with each other. You're right. I'm talking crazy."

"But I was talking about the fact that you were leaving the team."

"I'm still leaving. Can I send for you while I'm on the road?"

"NO!" she shrieked, getting out the bed and finding her robe near the bedroom door. "This isn't going to happen again. I'm a damn fool to let you even come here tonight."

"You're not a fool, Dana." He stood up and walked over to her.

She made no move to get away from him. As big as he was, he had never evoked fear in her. He didn't seem as if he was capable of hurting someone, yet there was this lurking Herculean power behind his eyes and movements. Maybe this was why Dana had always been attracted to him. He exuded a vigor supremacy that very few men could hold.

Her back was to the wall as he stood in front of her. He put his hands on each side of her head and leaned over her, but their bodies did not touch. The intensity of passion was in his eyes once more and Dana knew she would never deny this man anything.

"I think you're something special, Dana."

Damn! There he went again speaking to her heart. How the hell did he expect her not to fall in love with him even more if he continued to act like he really was in love with her?

"I think you're amazing," she admitted.

His kiss was brief, but it held so much emotion, she wanted to cry again.

A moment later, he was gone.

*   *   *   *   *

Awaking the next morning, she immediately saw the empty pillow beside her. Millions of mornings she had awakened to an empty pillow beside her, but for some reason this morning was different. The imprint of where his head had been was still there.

Moving over on the bed, she could smell his sweat, his odor – him. Her hands moved under the pillow to bury her face into the fabric, but she touched some paper. Raising the pillow to see what she was touching, she gasped at the large roll of money left.

She put the roll of money in the pocket of the robe and took a quick shower. The idea of him leaving money after they made love almost cheapened the experience. How could he do something like that?

So bothered by it even more after she got out the shower, she went over to her address book to see if she had a number for him. Dana could not ask her mother for the number, because she'd get too suspicious. Since she wouldn't be playing Denise anymore, she knew that she wouldn't be able to get the number from her sister without arousing suspicion.

Her doorbell rung and she ran to the door without looking to see who it was, hoping it was Jerome.

No such luck! Denise stood there looking like she had just stepped out of a salon.

"Good afternoon, Dana," Denise said, brushing past her and coming in Dana's home.

"Whatever it is," Dana said, closing the door and facing Denise, "The answer is no."

Denise feigned a look of shock. "What would make you think I want something?"

"Because for as long as I've been living here, you have never stepped foot on my property."

"I hadn't been invited."

"What about my house warming party? I *did* send you an invitation."

"You weren't serious about me coming, were you?" Denise took off her sunglasses and looked around. "It's so small. How could you have a party here?"

Her tone of disgust really rubbed Dana the wrong way. "The door is still unlocked, Denise. You can run your tail right on out. I've got work to do."

"It's eleven o'clock in the afternoon, Dana. What work do you have to do when you're about four hours late for it?"

Dana bit her lip to suppress the gasp. She usually was sitting at her computer by now and she had to get together her deliveries by five. In all the years of owning her business, she had never overslept. "I own my own business. I'm my own boss. I make my own hours."

The look of envy came over Denise's face. "Fine, Dana. Do we have time to talk?"

"Sure, but do you mind me getting dressed?"

Denise followed her sister to her bedroom door. "I wanted to first know how it went."

"How what went?" Dana was glad her sister stood outside the door because it gave Dana time to straighten the bed, before finding some clothes.

"My honeymoon, silly."

Dana quickly found a sweatshirt and pants, and then started to tackle her mused hair. "He didn't suspect a thing."

"Of course not. He's not an observant man, Dana. He just likes a pretty face."

That wasn't true about Jerome, in Dana's opinion. He was a confused man, but she wasn't going to dispute this with shallow Denise.

"Tell me what happened. He's bound to go down memory lane one day."

Talking about what happened on her honeymoon to someone she couldn't stand was rather sick, but Dana bit her lip again to remind herself that it wasn't all hers. True, Denise did not deserved Jerome, but Dana never felt from the get go that she deserved him either and if she ever wanted to be with him, her own deception had to be known. Once that was out the bag, Dana was positive Jerome would want nothing to do with her.

"I'm waiting," Denise said impatiently.

Dana had finished putting on her clothes and came out the room, headed toward the kitchen. Denise followed. "We got to the chapel/hotel, got married and spent the night together."

"What happened?! Did you fuck him?"

Dana quickly removed the two cups of coffee on the table, hoping Denise hadn't noticed them.

"No…I mean yes…this is way too embarrassing to discuss, Denise, and I couldn't deny him. There was some touching," she said evasively.

"What kind of touching?"

Dana warmed her water in the microwave to have some herbal tea and fixed her toast. "Tasting was more like it."

"Eww…you did that to him? He asked for it?"

"You never did that?"

"Once or twice," Denise admitted with an embarrassed cackle. "But he was so damn big my jaw got tired."

"Doesn't the idea of sharing your man with your sister bother you?"

"He's just a man," Denise said nonchalantly. "He's been shared before. Men do it all the time and don't think about it, Dana. There's nothing wrong with it. It's not like he was with both of us at the same time. Now that's nasty."

That was a weird way to accept the situation, but Dana had to admit she hadn't been thinking at all about Denise when Jerome was here last night making love to her. Yet, if there were two Jeromes she wouldn't mind being with them at the same time. This brought a slight amusement to herself.

"And then?" Denise asked.

Dana finished fixing her breakfast and went through the door that divided her flat with her office. Denise was right behind her.

"We slept, woke, went shopping, had lunch in Cleveland, came back, had sex somewhere between all that and then came home."

"And?"

"And what? That's it."

"And how was he?"

"I mean he was a good lover-"

Disgusted, Denise said, "I'm not talking about in bed. I mean how was he as a person, silly."

"Jerome's a nice guy. He was nothing but nice."

"Oh please, the man's got a tongue that lays people low. He's crude and sarcastic all the time."

They were talking about two different people in Dana's opinion. "Look, Denise. Jerome was nothing but nice to me. I'm not lying."

Denise huffed, while digging around in his purse. "Here's the money I promised you."

Dana looked at the check her sister handed her. It was twenty thousand. "This is more than we discussed."

"I know, but your services are not done, Dana." Denise handed her another envelope.

"What's that?"

"It's a plane ticket to sunny Florida."

"You're giving me a vacation?" Dana asked suspiciously.

"Yes and no, silly." Denise sat in a nearby chair, as Dana sat behind her desk and logged into her computer. "I'm giving you an opportunity to be with him again."

"What?" Dana almost dropped her tea all over her desk.

"He left this morning to go to spring training early, but he ordered me to have my ass in Miami in August to our vacation home down there in a month before the season starts and I had better act like I had acted on our honeymoon. I've never stayed at the home personally, but it used to be the home where he grew up before he moved up here. I know it's only to come down there and have sex because he doesn't like to have sex while the season is going on. That's why I came over to find all that out. Seems like he's not going to take my attitude anymore and I can't think of any more ways to put him off anymore. Since I can't think of ways to disobey my husband-"

Dana cut her off correcting her, "He's *my* husband, remember?"

Denise sucked her teeth. "Oh yeah. Well, I was on my way to my lawyers anyway to discuss that matter, but since you enjoyed yourself the first time being me, why not again?" Denise said with a hint of her own special brand of nastiness.

"NO!" Dana exclaimed, standing up and handing her the check. "And I don't want your money. Not anymore."

"Oh please," Denise said sarcastically. "You need the money. Look at this dump!"

Dana tore up the check and hurled the shreds at her sister. "Get the hell out my house, Denise."

Standing up, Denise shrugged. "I can write another check. Think about it. It's not for another month, Dana."

"Get out!"

Denise left and Dana slumped in the chair distraught.

Part 14

For several weeks Dana avoided Denise's phone calls. The more time passed, the more of a slump she fell into. Jerome never contacted her and she started to worry because her perfectly timed fail to start as expected.

When she was almost two weeks late, she really started to worry and went to the store to get a pregnancy test.

Just as she was reading the positive results her doorbell rung.

Andre stood at the door with an outstretched white envelope and a look of concern on his face.

"Are you all right?"

She didn't answer. The queasiness in her stomach had started again and she found herself sprinting to the bathroom and throwing up the toast and tea she had that morning.

He had entered the house and was standing at the bathroom entrance as she continued to regurgitate the contents of last night's dinner.

"Looks like you had some food that didn't agree with you. You need me to call an ambulance or something?" he asked when she finally stopped.

Dana shook her head and rinsed her mouth out with water before taking a swig of mouthwash. After clearing her throat, she asked, "What are you doing here?"

"Denise was concerned."

"And?"

"Well, she said she knew if she came, you probably wouldn't let her in and if Gloria came, you probably wouldn't listen, so she thought I could do something. Help, you know?"

"Help me with what?"

"She said what's ever in the envelope you would know."

Looking down at the envelope, she saw the words, "You owe me," written on the front in Denise's handwriting. Opening the envelope she found another check for twenty thousand, plane tickets and directions to get to Jerome's summer home. There was a security card at the bottom of the envelope as well.

Andre continued to speak as she stared at the envelope's contents.

"She said to tell you that she spoke with a lawyer and when you return, she'll have some papers sent over for you to sign. Papers that will release you from whatever she had you get into. She wouldn't tell me the details, but she said you would understand. The only thing will be that the papers won't be submitted until the end of the year."

Dana needed to go. She wanted to see him, but…

Turning away from Andre to gather her thoughts, she clutched the envelope. All the deceit through out the years overcame her, bringing tears to her eyes and she didn't know if she could ever tell Jerome the truth.

"You okay, Dana?" Andre asked concerned.

"Yeah," she said tightly. "I'll be okay. Tell her, I'll do it."

*   *   *   *   *

Finding the small townhouse Jerome Lott owned wasn't very hard once she gave the cab driver the address. Dana had planned to get a rental from the airport, but she had decided to that as option only if needed. Although Denise had given her a three-day window before her departure flight, Dana had no real intentions of staying.

One night with Jerome and then she would go. She just needed to get what she should have already had as his 'wife', a telephone number.

The house was just as beautiful as the one in Michigan. The master bedroom's walk-in closet was filled with an array of clothing, some items with price tags still intact. The bed was a California king, but looked more like a conjoined king and twin. She also found a trophy room with all his pre-college stuff and of course a private workout room. In the home's rear was an Olympic size pool and a private area four-person Jacuzzi. .

She noticed a nice sized guesthouse a short walk past the pool and felt drawn to go and look around. When Dana's security card failed to open either of the two entranceways, she was forced to peek through the windows. It was obvious someone was occupying the space; the closet was open and men's clothing were hanging inside.

She knocked on the door and rung the doorbell, but no one answered. Moving around the other side of the guesthouse, she saw there was another trophy room, but she could barely see the name on the trophies. Luckily she spotted a trophy placed near one of the windows that read, "T. Lott." It couldn't have belonged to Jerome's father since his first name was Artie.

The flight had left her exhausted and given her 'condition' she decided to get some rest. It was ten in the morning and although she was famished she knew eating was not a good idea, but instead a nap was her best bet.

She awoke hours later, to find an envelop on the bed. She opened it and saw that there was a V.I.P. pass to the game with Miami and Detroit at seven o'clock that night. There was a short note in Jerome's handwriting. "Limo pick up at six."

Dana wondered if he had come or had someone else delivered the package. Getting out of bed, she saw there was a second set of suitcases by hers and she knew someone had been in the room.

Opening up the first bag, she immediately smelled Jerome's scent and instinctively knew these were his items. Just as she was about to close the bag, she noticed a boarding pass sticking out the bag. The name on the ticket was T.J. Lott.

Sticking the ticket back in its place, she showered, put on the type of make-up Denise would wear and then found the most expensive outfit in the closet. The three thousand dollar price tag was still on it and Dana almost had a heart attack, but she quickly recovered and found matching shoes.

The limo arrived on time and took her through one of the stadium's private entrances, showed her V.I.P. card and was escorted to a suite filled with food, a comfortable seating area and a large window where one could view the whole stadium. There were also tickets that would allow her to sit in the stands if she desired.

Soon as the attendant left her alone, she went over to the food and found something light to eat knowing it would come back up in the morning. After her third bottle of water, she promised herself she'd make an appointment to see her doctor when she returned home.

The door opened and Jerome filled the doorway with his massive frame. He looked even bigger and sexier in his uniform.

He stepped in and closed the door. "I didn't think you were coming."

She turned away not really knowing how to be Denise with him when she just wanted to leap in his arms and kiss him.

"I made arrangements. I felt I should be here since you asked nicely."

He snorted derogatively. "I didn't ask nicely."

"I was being sarcastic."

Dana could feel him moving toward her and slightly jumped when he dropped his helmet on the floor. As powerful as he was, she sensed the insecurity he was desperately trying to hide.

Turning to face, he looked stone cold, but as he gazed into her eyes, she saw how he instantly softened. "Hey, D," he said before he lovingly took her into his arms and kissed her.

She tried to stiffen, but his warm mouth penetrated her lips and heart.

"I missed you, so damn much." His arms tightened so much, she thought her spine would crack, but she loved it.

"I missed you too."

"Say it," he ordered, nibbling on her ear.

"I love you, Jerome."

That bright smile returned to his lips and she was butter in his arms. "Do you really, D?"

"Yes, I do."

He kissed her again. This time more passionately, with a promise for more.

There was a knock on the door and Jerome reluctantly drew away and picked up his helmet. "You'll stay for the whole game?"

"Yes!" she promised, giddy as a schoolgirl.

"I could get you a little cheerleader outfit," he said wickedly.

"Shut up and go before you get in trouble."

After a playful wink and a pat on her ass, he was gone. She missed him all over again. Why couldn't she see this horrible side that Denise saw. What made her bring out this wonderful man?

The Lions won the game and Jerome played well. Every time he was tackled, she was biting her lip. She even went out in the stands to watch the game more closely and cheered along with the fans.

It was fun doing so, because in high school, she had to cheer for her school when he visited.

He was standing on the sideline and as soon as she was seated, he turned to her and they made eye contact. At first she thought he was going to run up in the stands and kiss her, but he only nodded.

It felt so good to know he acknowledged her and she felt like they were in high school, but this time she was his sweetheart and her heart soared.   This man was hers and he had claimed her heart a long time ago.

After the game, an attendant came to escort her down to team's locker room. When she walked in he was putting on his jacket and she was introduced to the whole team. Some of them had been at the wedding, but that day had been so hectic and mesmerizing for her, she hadn't remembered some of them.

Jerome was a totally different person around his teammates and she saw a lot of sarcasm and manliness, but still adorable.

"Want dinner?" he asked, as they headed toward the limousine.

"Just a little. Can we just grab something and go back home?" she asked.

He smiled. "I like the way you say that, D."

They picked up Chinese on the way home. She took the food inside while he paid the driver. When he came in, she had placed the food on the coffee table.

Dana lit some candles and Jerome started a fire before sitting on the floor next to her. "Aren't you worried about your clothes?"

She knew Denise would never sit on the floor in a three thousand dollar outfit. "I'll go up and change."

He pulled her under him and popped the first button on her shirt. "I'll buy you ten outfits if you don't."

She didn't even know if she responded to his offer, because he was busy kissing her and tearing off the rest of her clothes. Amazed by his power yet gentleness, Dana let his enthusiasm encompass her and rival him.

Every inch of his skin on was adorned by her kisses, rolling him onto his stomach she delved into his crack, licking the masculine taste of him. At first Jerome was skeptical, but as she swirled her tongue around the dark opening, his shaft increased in size and he was gripping the brightly colored Tibetan rug in strained excitement.

He rolled over to his back and she pressed hard on the skin between his balls with her thumb and anus as she put his dick in the back of her mouth. His ejaculation almost choked her as it shot down her throat, but his hard on didn't disappear and she found she had opened up a new level of sexual stimulation for him.

By one in the morning, she was so exhausted; she didn't think she could raise an eyelid more less a muscle. But somehow they had eaten and made it upstairs to the bedroom.

Part 15

They cocooned until dawn and she slept like a log until she smelled the aroma of hot pancakes, bacon and eggs. The scent sent her running for the bathroom.

By the time he came up with the tray of food, she had locked the bathroom door and was running water to disguise the nauseating sounds.

"D, you okay?"

Too busy reliving last night meal, Dana didn't answer.

"Open the door," he ordered knocking.

"No," she said, holding back a heave.

There was a moment of silence, but she knew he was still at the door. She hurriedly rinsed her mouth out with water and swigged mouthwash.

"Open the door or I'll break it down," he ordered.

At first she was tempted to see if he could. Then she remembered last night's game when Miami intercepted Detroit's ball during a second and goal drive. Jerome tackled the corner back so hard the guy did a back flip. Dana's heart leaped as Jerome caught the ball and ran it back for a thirty-five yard touch down.

A simple wooden door and her hundred and forty pound body pressed up against it, probably wouldn't stop that man from coming through.

"You're going to have to do better than that to stop me," he said as if reading her thoughts.

She opened the door partially and glared up at him, angry that he could read her so easily. "What's your problem?"

"I don't like locked doors. Especially in my house."

"Our house," she corrected him. "I'm married to you, which means I own half."

"Why is the door locked?"

"I was busy washing up."

"Are you ashamed to be naked in front of me?" he asked incredulously.

"Are you accusing me of something, Jerome?"

He slammed the tray on the polished wooden floor and pushed open the door making her stumble back away from it. The bathroom was clean and free of any evidence.

"Where's your precious phone, Denise?" he sneered.

"In my purse, downstairs." Hitting him his steel chest, which only hurt her wrist.

"You're being an insecure ass. I wasn't doing anything, now get out." She rubbed her wrist.

His look of apology was instant and he took her wrist to examine it. "I'm sorry. I just love you too much, D."

"I know."

He pulled her into his arms and she fought the urge not to heave.

"I'll fix you some more food."

It took every ounce of strength not to throw up. Pushing away from him, she went to the sink, grabbed a disposable cup and ran some much needed cold water.

"No, I'm fine. I don't think the food we ate last night agreed with me." This was partially true. The food last night didn't agree with the baby.

"Is there anything I can do?"

She shook her head and kept her back to him. If she opened her mouth one more time, she would definitely hurl.

He walked out the room, closed the door behind him and cleaned up the mess from the tray, while she forced herself to keep it together.

Dana knew if she could hold out for another ten minutes, she would be fine, but until then she had to hold it together.

Once her morning sickness passed, she was right as rain. She put on clothes and when she came out, he was already dressed, sitting in the kitchen cove finishing up the new breakfast he'd cooked for them.

"What's that guest house for?" she asked, trying to draw him into a subject that wasn't uncomfortable.

"Nothing," he snipped.

She couldn't tell if he was angry with her or not.

"Can we go out?" she asked.

"To do what?"

"Go somewhere."

Raising a brow, he asked thinking that he knew the obvious location, "Shopping?"

She had a feeling that would be Denise's response, but she didn't want to go shopping.

"I've never been to Florida before."

"Yes, we have. We use to come here all the time to visit my parents during college vacations or whenever I could get away. Not this house, but their new home in Tallahassee they purchased after my brother and I went away to college."

"You have a brother?" she slipped out.

"Stop playing dumb." He looked rather offended.

"So those are your brother's things in the guesthouse?"

He cleaned off the table and said, "I'm going out by myself."

Dana didn't want him to leave angry, so she called out to him in desperation. He instantly stopped at the doorway, but didn't turn around to face her.

"I'm sorry," she said. "I just wasn't feeling well."

"You're never feeling well around me."

"I want to spend the day with you, like we did on our honeymoon."

He turned around to face her.

"You're driving me nuts. I don't know how to be around you."

"How do you want to be around me, Jerome?'

At a loss for words, he huffed in frustration. "I don't know. I want to be me."

Cautiously, she moved up to him. "Then be yourself."

He took her hand and led her out the room. There was a car in the garage and he drove her around Tampa, the nearby city and Dana had the time of her life.

By the time they returned home with bags of stuff, they fell asleep wrapped up in each other's arms on the couch. Her bout of sickness hit her really early in the next morning but didn't last as long. After she washed up and lay back down, an hour later they made love again, slowly as if every second was to be embedded into their memories.

He had to leave in the afternoon for a team meeting, but returned shortly after and she found herself in bed with him again. He seemed refreshed and enthusiastic all over again as if he hadn't just made love to her hours ago.

By nightfall, she awoke in the bed alone and decided to cook something for them, but she wanted to find him and let him know her intentions.

He wasn't in the house, so she checked the backyard. There were lights on in the guesthouse and she was positive she heard two voices coming from that direction.

"Jerome," she called.

A door slammed and he appeared at her side out of nowhere. Kissing her, he smiled mischievously.

"I didn't tire you out did I?"

She giggled wickedly. "You almost did, but I'm starving."

"You should be, you haven't eaten a good meal in almost two days. Are you okay?"

"Yes," she assured him and then looked at the guesthouse again. The lights were out, but she was sure they had been on just seconds ago.

"Do we have guests?"

"No, the lights are on a timer," he answered and drew her into the house.

Dana dropped the subject and let him lead her in the house where they found something to eat on and then ended right back up in bed.

Since they had slept through the afternoon, they were both wide-awake.

"You aren't pregnant, are you?" he asked suddenly when she had come from the bathroom and lay back in bed with him again.

She paused for a moment very tempted to spill the beans, but then decided against it.

"No, do you want me to be?"

"Hell, yeah," he said.

Giggling at his exuberance in the matter, she spilled out, "Denise wouldn't like that."

There was a moment of quietness in the room.

Dana quickly corrected herself.

"You know, the *bitchy* Denise, the part you don't like about me."

Jerome relaxed a little.

"Yeah, her," he agreed and kissed her.

She relaxed as he drew her against him.

"Are you cheating on me, Jerome?" she asked suddenly. She really didn't know why she was asking and knew this would most likely put them back on the outs.

He took a moment before he said, "Yes."

His honesty shocked her and she didn't know how to respond. "How long? With whom?"

"Does it matter? I thought I was spending this weekend with my wife? You asked a question and I had to be honest with you. I can't lie to you, D."

Pushing away and sitting up, she looked at him.

"Do you love her?"

He sat up.

"Please, D. Don't ask questions that you can never possibly understand. I don't understand it. We all have reasons why we cheat, don't we? Have you ever been in love with two people?"

She didn't know how to answer this again without sounding like herself. Denise would get up and leave or make him leave, wouldn't she?

"I want to leave," she said suddenly.

He got out the bed without protest.

"I'll take you to the airport."

"Could you go down and get me a bottle of water?" she asked suddenly.

When he was out the room, she went over to his cell phone by the bedside table and took his number down. Since he hadn't returned, she scrolled through his phone book. There was no one besides his teammates, coaches, some business numbers, a few friends including Andre and Gloria that were at the wedding, his parents, Denise's cell phone and then there was a person listed as TJ's cell. The area code was three-one-three, which meant that this TJ lived in Detroit or in its surrounding area.

He was coming back up the stairs and she quickly put the cell phone down. Going over to her bags, she pulled her jacket out and sat in a chair.

Handing her the water, he said, "I don't want you to go."

Looking up at him, she had a million and one questions to ask him, but if she did, she wouldn't be Denise. No, she had to make him angry enough to stay away.

"Take me to the airport, Jerome," she said just above a whisper.

He grabbed his clothes and went to the bathroom. She sighed reluctantly.

Part 16

As soon as Dana returned home, she went on a fact-finding mission via the Internet. She was able to research a little of Jerome's history. In high school down in Florida, he surpassed a lot of sports records and still kept a perfect G.P.A. He was an accomplished swimmer, baseball player and also played classical piano, before coming up here in his eleventh grade year in high school and finishing off in Detroit, valedictorian of his class. At South Florida A&M, before he transferred to Michigan, he still had a perfect G.P.A. and was able to still excel in at least four top sports. Even when he came to Michigan, he kept up the progress.

This was unique. Good players were good at one thing, but not at all things. Jerome was simply good at everything!

Dana did a search on T.J. Lott. The closest she came was finding a Tyrone Lott that played in the European league, but that was it. There were no pictures on the Internet and there was no history on him. He played for two seasons, did some amazing stuff and then two years ago went into oblivion.

After catching up on work, she found a good movie to watch and let the television put her to sleep. She had taken a Lions' season schedule and knew the first home game wasn't until the middle of September. By then she would be over two months pregnant.

During her initial doctor's visit, they confirmed she was pregnant, but the doctor seemed to have some reservations about the pregnancy. Her urine had produced some strange test results, so he told her to come back before her third month to run some more tests.

Dana was attending a medical billing conference was in Chicago the week of Jerome's first home game so she knew she missed him. When she returned home Tuesday morning, she found roses on her doorstep and a phone number on the card that read, "I just want to talk."

She called the number and was surprised that a woman picked up. "Marriott Hotel Detroit, how may I help you?"

"Jerome Lott, please."

"One moment." There were several clicks before he came on the line.

"Dana?" he asked.

"Yes," she said.

He sighed with relief. "Come to me."

"No."

"It's not a request, Dana."

"I'm not your wife, Jerome. You can't order me around."

He chuckled. "Then come to piss her off."

She laughed this time. "I won't do that either."

"Even if I told you I really need you?"

The man had a weakness for her and she enjoyed the power she had over him. "Twelve."

"Thank you, Dana."

Hanging up, she smiled to herself. This was crazy, but she was actually going to see him.

Arriving at the hotel, she was promptly met and escorted to a private elevator.

When the doors opened again, Jerome was waiting with open arms as she stepped off the lift and into a much needed hug.

She broke the embrace, she looked up at him, and she slapped him as hard as she could.

"What the hell was that for?!" he exclaimed.

She reached in her pocket threw a roll of bills at him. "Don't you ever leave money at my home like I'm your private hoe, Jerome."

"I was trying to help, Dana! Dammit! I knew you wouldn't take the money if I gave it to you straight up."

"I don't want anything from you, Jerome!" she cried exasperated. "Why would you think I would want something from you?"

"Because all I've ever given you was myself. It didn't seem enough. You deserve so much more and money is what I could give." He pulled her in his arms even though she resisted, but soon she allowed him to mold her body against his.

She pushed away slightly and looked up in apology. "That hurts, Jerome."

At first he looked a bit reserved, but then he looked down at her stomach and his eyes widened as he realized the fullness of her breast and body.

"You're pregnant?!"

Dana nodded.

Dropping to his knees, he kissed her stomach. "When? How long, Dana?"

His concern overwhelmed her and she was truly touched by all the questions he asked her.

As they had lunch on a terrace, he seemed really put out that he hadn't been there from the beginning.

"Dammit, Dana, I'd quit right now to spend more time with you."

"Jerome, might I remind you that I'm your sister-in-law and that we can't go on like this?"

Reserved sitting back, he nodded. "I'll divorce her."

"To be with your child? No, Jerome, that won't work for me." Though it was selfish, Dana didn't want him to do anything unless he was doing it for her.

Leaning forward on the table, he declared, "I'll divorce her to be with you, Dana. I've been doing a lot of thinking and I figure if I can't have the woman I fell in love with all the time, then I'll be satisfied with the woman who loves me."

"But you don't love me, Jerome."

"I'm honest with you, Dana. I can't help it that I lost my heart to her a long time ago, but I have a feeling I won't ever get her back. She's too far gone."

"What do you mean?"

"She hasn't been to the house. The whole time I was on the road, she hasn't been living there."

"Where has she been living?"

"Your guess is as good as mine, but I have some ideas."

She was a bit shocked and decided to shift the conversation to relieve some of the tension.

"So why are you here and not at home?"

"I often take a suite here to be in the city and I didn't think it was very appropriate to stay at your place."

Dana smiled and got up from the table. "We'll figure out the baby situation together, Jerome."

"I don't want anymore time to pass. You'll be having my baby."

"*Our* baby," she corrected. She left off the terrace feeling confuse and frustrated, but unable to say anything to him when she wanted to share everything with him.

He followed her into the front room.

"What's on your mind, Dana?"

"You, Jerome. You're always on my mind. And I don't want you to divorce my sister and I don't want her to know about the pregnancy. And I want you to go on about your career, or whatever you want to do with your life and we can just arrange for you to see the child whenever you want."

He looked extremely baffled. "That's it? That's all you'll settle for?"

"Yes, that's all I can settle for."

"Dana-"

She cut him off. "Don't try to convince me of something different, something better between us, because it can't happen. Even if you left her, it will never be there because of what I've –"

She stopped herself and covered her mouth. He would never forgive her if he knew the truth.

Jerome pulled her into his arms. "Fine, Dana. Whatever you want." Kissing her brow, he rubbed her back to comfort her.

The rest of the day was pleasant, but by seven, someone began calling his until Dana decided she needed to leave.

"Before this gets ugly, I should leave," she said, writing down as she had promised the name of her doctor and the next appointment date.

He wrote his cell phone number on a hotel notepad and told her to call him. She promised, not admitting she already had his cell number.

Upon getting home, she found Denise standing at her door about to leave a Post-It on her mailbox.

"You haven't answered your phone since you've been back."

"I do answer my phone, I just don't answer your calls, Denise."

"Are you trying to say you don't like me, Dana?" she asked sarcastically amused.

"I'm trying to say that I'm not in the mood to try to hear anything you have to say. Stay away from my property, Denise, and me. We have nothing to speak about anymore." Dana went into the house and Denise followed.

"Dana, did you think it was going to be over so soon?"

Facing her twin, she said, "What's that suppose to mean?"

"It means I need you again. He needs that nice loving person that I just can't pretend to be anymore for him."

"Why don't you just leave him? Why do you have to save face for some sorority sisters, who could give a fig's ass about you, Denise?"

"They are *my* soros and I'm not going to let you talk about them that way."

"You never stopped them from talking about me. You are a shallow bitch."

Denise slapped her.

Dana stepped back holding her face.

Taking off her sunglasses, Denise glared at her. "I'm only doing what's best for us, Dana. I'm giving you the chance to stop fantasizing and I'm giving me a chance to have what I always wanted."

"And what's that, Denise?"

"Everything, I deserve."

Dana turned her back on her.

"He wants me to come to Washington, D.C. for an after Thanksgivings football thing."

"I can't." She would definitely be showing by then.

"Yes, you will," Denise said adamantly. She placed the plane ticket on the table. "There'll be a limo for Mrs. Lott when you step off the plane. There's a wives' dinner before the game they always have during the season. You'll go and attend as me, while I spend my time in the Bahamas."

"With your lover?"

"Yes, Dana. With my lover," Denise answered, annoyed.

"Who is he?"

"None of your concern. Like I said, he makes me happy."

Dana asked trying to hold back a sob of misery, "Doesn't Jerome?"

"His money gives me the luxury of spending time with my lover." Denise put on her sunglasses and prepared to leave.

"Why can't you just stop this?"

"I promised you at the end of this season. Do you know Jerome's playing better than he's ever played? He signed a two-year contract with the Lions and now the Redskins are looking at him quite favorably. I'm thinking by next year, he'll sign a five-year deal with them for at least twenty million. Can you just imagine that?"

"No, I can't."

"Oh, and just so you don't think you can just shuffle some silly paper on my face, why don't you take a look at this piece of art work."

Dana looked down at the Toledo marriage certificate with Denise's name on it. Tears welled up in her eyes and she let the paper drop to the floor.

"I could always tell Jerome the truth. I'm sure you'll live happily ever after knowing that he's had a stalker his whole life, won't he? That's right after he gets a restraining order out on your ass."

"Get out," Dana hissed disgusted by guilt and her sister.

Denise left with a sinister chuckle.

*   *   *   *   *

During November, her fourth month, she was finding that it was getting more and more difficult to hide her pregnancy. She was surprised that she was showing so much when other women told her that they didn't show until six months. Jerome came to every appointment faithfully. She had them planned around his game schedule and he would fly in just to go in to the doctor's office with her and then leave out.

Yet, sometimes he would come back, right after a game from out of town and be with her sooner than expected. And he would avoid her questions about the time he spent with her and getting in trouble at home with his wife.

Dana tried not to think about it. With him playing, he was adamant about not having sex, but that didn't stop him from tasting her, showering with her, and tantalizing her with massages. Plus, the doctor had said there seemed to be some trouble with the pregnancy, but there was really no real cause for alarm until the four-month appointment.

The doctor had scheduled her four-month appointment the day before the home Thanksgiving game with the Green Bay Packers. She was waiting for test results to come in from her doctor's concern.

Jerome entered the office just as her name was being called. He followed her in after a brief hug.

"How are you?" she asked.

"I'm great," he said just as cordially. "I want us to talk after this."

"I have a meeting," she lied.

"No, you don't. Admit it, Dana, you're not a good liar."

The doctor cleared his throat and they watched the screen as the doctor spoke. He was rolling the scanner over her stomach so they could both see inside her belly. This would be the first time they would actually see the life they had created.

Jerome held her hand and her heart instantly warmed at his tenderness and concern. The fact that he was sharing this moment with her was just amazing in itself.

"Just as the test results predicted," the doctor said. "This explains everything, Dana."

She peered at the screen closely and Jerome said out loud what she saw.

"Twins?"

"Yes," the doctor confirmed moving the scanner again. "Would you care to know the sex?"

They both nodded affirmatively.

"Boys."

Jerome tightened his grip and smiled.

After her stomach was wiped off and she was thoroughly checked out, the doctor asked if Jerome could step out the room for a moment.

When she was alone with the doctor, he said, "I had some reservations about this pregnancy, Dana, because of some early results with your urine. After running some tests, my concerns were correct. Are you sure you want me to speak freely about this in front of him?"

Dana frowned. Why would the doctor feel that way? "Is it something that concerns the babies?" She held her stomach protectively.

"The babies seem healthy, but they have two different DNA's."

She frowned harder. "I don't know what you mean. You mean they have my DNA and his?"

"No, Dana. The babies both have your DNA, but two different men fathered each child."

Part 17

"Two men?" she repeated in amazement. "That's impossible. I've only been with one man."

He pulled up some funny looking charts and hung them on the X-ray reader. "Not if they were brothers, Dana. My guess, twins. And since we were able to see two different strands of DNA, I would even go so far as to say they're fraternal twins" The doctor saw the shock on her face.

"And by the look of your face, you didn't know, so I can assume that they look exactly alike with some minor differences that you had not picked up on."

Her mouth dropped open. Who had been pulling the wool over whose eyes?

"Twins?" she asked to be sure.

"Does he have a brother?"

"Yes, but he never talks about him. The guesthouse in Florida," she said more to herself than her doctor.

"Do you want him to come in?" the doctor asked.

"No. Can I call you back when I have more information about what's going on?"

"Sure, anytime. What do you suspect?"

"That I'm a fool and Jerome Lott's got a lot of explaining to do." She put on her clothes and left out the room.

Jerome stood as she walked out. He was holding her jacket and purse and ending a call on his cell.

Although it took every ounce of restraint not to scream at him in the lobby, she waited until they were in the parking lot alone.

"You're keeping secrets!"

He was at a lost for words, but then the realization sunk in and he took her arm. She tried to snatch away, but he held on tightly and pulled her over to a staircase where their voices could not be heard.

"And what secrets are you keeping from me?" he shot back.

"Don't you dare turn the tables on me, Jerome," she sneered, hitting his chest.

"Dammit, you've got a twin."

"What makes you think that?"

"The doctor said it."

He chuckled. "A twin? And what? He's been taking my place, Dana?"

In a way it did sound like she was talking crazy. If Jerome had a twin, wouldn't she have known? Wouldn't Denise have known?

"What makes you think that?" Jerome asked. "Because you've been switching places with your twin?"

She turned her back to him. "You're crazy. You're always talking crazy."

"How long?" he demanded.

Gawd, she was never a good liar.

"How long what?"

He angrily slammed his fist against the wall and Dana jumped a little.

"How long have you pretending to be her, Dana?!"

Facing him, she shrugged as if it didn't matter.

"What does it matter? You love her. You've always loved her. No matter what, you could have never been mine."

"You would have never known that."

"You were in love with a face, not a person!"

"I was in love with the girl I saw at my games. The girl who watched and loved me from afar. Was that you all along, Dana?"

"Yes," she admitted, knowing this would be the deciding moment in the future of their relationship.

"Why?"

The truth burst from her lips. "Because the first time I saw you, I thought you were the most magnificent man I ever saw."

"But you didn't know me. You didn't know anything about me."

"It didn't matter."

He calmed down and forced her to look up at him. "So tell me, Dana, was that you at the park as well?"

"Yes, it was me." She began to spill her beans. Everything! If she lost him, she would at least have a clear conscious about it.

He took her hand gently in his and led her out the parking structure. Nearby was a park. As they walked over there and sat down, she spoke about everything. How she'd followed him and watched him. How she would just stand outside his window when she was younger just to gaze at him. How he would sneak out the house and party a lot and how she realized how his underage drinking really affected him.

Then he spotted Denise at one of the games and put a little of it together by asking people about Denise. Dana knew she had to get to him before he talked to Denise, so she followed him to the party one night and got off the bus and watched him in the park.

He came out the party and spotted her. She knew she had to make him swear never to bring it up and he kept his promises until he drunk so much from a party in college and told Denise about that night.

Still after she met him again, Dana couldn't tell him what she had been doing.

"Denise has always gotten what she wanted and she wanted you. I've never had the strength to fight her. And I've failed to fulfill a lot of my dreams. So I just accepted that you could have never been mine to begin with, Jerome."

"That doesn't mean she deserves me, Dana," he said. "All you had to do was admit it. That's it."

She stood up and held her stomach protectively. "And then what? We would have lived happily ever after? This still doesn't explain what the doctor told me, Jerome."

"And what did he say?" Jerome asked, standing behind her.

"He said that there are two fathers. He suspected brothers. He suspected fraternal twins that looked a lot alike. So much so their physical differences wouldn't be that noticeable." She turned to him and didn't falter as she looked up in his eyes.

"I've told you everything, Jerome. Now tell me everything."

He cupped her shoulders and held her close, looking into her eyes as if it would tell him more. "You ever loved two people at one time, Dana?"

"Why do you keep asking me that? Because you love Denise and I?"

"No, because we both love you." He turned her around and forced her to face the street, where a tall man seemed to distance himself from the crowd and head in their direction.

As he approached, Dana's eyes widened as she realized Jerome's face was on another man. Yet, he had a slightly smaller build. Suddenly blackness surrounded Dana as the man stood just inches away. A man was certain was Jerome's fraternal twin.

Part 18

When she opened her eyes she immediately realized she wasn't in a hospital, but the hotel suite. Instinctively, she touched her stomach, feeling reasonably assured her babies were fine.

Sitting up, she still felt a little dizzy, but if she paced herself, she would be fine. Pulling the covers aside, she eased off bed. Someone had removed her shoes and placed them across the room near her purse and coat.

It looked as if it was late in the day, but she couldn't be sure.

The bedroom door was slightly ajar and she became aware of the voices in the other room. Instantly, she recognized her doctor's voice.

Moving quietly, she listened closely and then peered into the room. They were sitting in the front room. Jerome and his twin were sitting on the couch across from her doctor. She wasn't aware her doctor made house calls, but she was positive Jerome had offered him enough money to encourage this change in procedure.

"It is very rare that twins have two different fathers, but what I suspect is that if the both of you had intercourse with her about the same day and within the same time frame of six to twelve hours, then I would bet it would be possible," her doctor said.

Jerome looked at his brother and the both of them had the nerve to smile.

"Doc, when do you think she got pregnant?" T.J. asked.

"I'd say late July, early August. We're never really sure." He pulled out a circular calendar to determine from her last cycle. "My closest guess would be sometime in July."

Jerome and T.J. simultaneous said, "The wedding."

Dana had come to the same conclusion and cursed herself for even thinking the same thoughts as these deceitful, dishonest bastards.

Standing up, the doctor said, "I really must go. She should be fine."

"Thank you, doctor," Jerome said and passed the doctor a couple hundred dollars. "This should cover the expense."

While the other man walked the doctor out, Jerome headed for the bedroom.

She scrambled to the bed and pretended to be sleep, cracking her eye just a little to watch the doorway.

"Jerome, she's not going to wake up with you watching her," T.J. said.

"Dammit, TJ, I told you this was not the way," Jerome said upset, stepping away from the door. "We should have told her a long time ago."

"Told who? Denise or Dana? If you mean, Denise, then you were out of your mind. I knew something wasn't right."

"Denise was fine, until you opened up your big drunk mouth. We could never get Denise back after you revealed that night."

Jerome was quiet for a moment, but said, "We didn't even know about the other twin until she brought us home from college. She had kept it a secret. Still, I knew it was someone else all along. I just didn't know about Dana until we met her."

"But we didn't know about the deceit they were playing us for until after we got Dana down to Toledo."

The other one chuckled. "I think it's amusing. Almost hilarious." He looked fondly at the bed. "You've got to admit, with all the shuffling, she was damn good."

Jerome chuckled too and looked at the bed affectionately. "I didn't know she'd get pregnant, though."

"And I didn't know this different daddy shit could happen. Damn!"

"So what should we do?"

"Follow the original plan, bro. That's the only thing to do. Let that bitch continue to think we're staying with her. Denise will keep her fucking mouth close when we threatened to let her little soros know how she blackmailed her sister."

Dana almost wanted to smile, but continued to remain perfectly still. She was digging this T.J., but she was still upset at the both of them.

"T.J., we were wrong to deceive Dana like this," Jerome said. "We're going to have to do some mad apologizing."

There was a moment of silence as each man deliberated his deception all the while looking at her.

T.J. glanced at his watch and said, "You've got to get going, J. She'll be fine with me."

"I wanted to be here when she wakes up. I want to know she'll be all right."

"The doctor said she'd be fine. You'll be late. I can handle her. Haven't I done that before?"

Reluctantly, Jerome left and Dana knew she was not going to give them a chance to explain anything. They had nothing to say to her because there was nothing she wanted to hear from either of them. Dana was way past angry from this whole deception, despite the fact that she had deceived them initially.

When a few hours passed and all she heard from the outer room was silence, she got up and crept to the doorway. T.J. had fallen asleep over some paperwork. She grabbed her shoes, her coat and purse and tiptoed out the suite.

She took a cab to her doctor's office and found her car. Quickly, she drove home forcing herself not to think just to avoid crying out of frustration. After getting home, she locked her door, pulled the shades and disabled the ringers on both her phones.

Someone knocked on her door, but she didn't answer. She didn't go to the door.

"I know you're in there, Dana. Fuck! Open the door!"

It was Jerome's voice, but she knew it was actually T.J. The cell phone number on Jerome's phone and the trophies now all made sense.

He went away after a while, but came back about eleven that night and then both of them came back about three in the morning.

When she checked her cell phone, there were over twenty voicemails, which she didn't even bother to listen to. She just deleted them.

Looking at her calendar, she knew she was planning on a lot of things to be in her favor. She was fully stocked with food and the only person due to come around her place was the FedEx man, but she could leave her packages outside the door for pickup.

That could last for a couple of weeks before she had to leave the house again.

The way she felt at the moment she never wanted to see Jerome or his dirty rotten brother again.

*   *   *   *   *

The roses started arriving a week after Thanksgiving. Two dozens each time delivered by two different companies at the same time each week. Roses were costly during the wintertime – she knew this if nothing else and to admit she was impressed by the gesture.

Denise called several times and even came by, but Dana didn't open her door. She had started to show and she didn't want anyone to see her, especially her family.

Dana refused the flowers the first two weeks, but when she received a delivery for Christmas, she lowered her guard and accepted them since they were the closest things to a gift she had received. After that, she allowed them to come and put them on her desk. Often she would gaze at them while she worked. Her mind was going a million miles a minute. Two brothers. Two men. Both willing to make her happy. Both handsome. Both great in bed.

Why hadn't she realized the differences until now? The physical differences, once she thought about it were slight. Jerome was much thicker, while T.J. was cut. T.J. had darker brown eyes and hair than his brother and his lips were thicker. Jerome was easy going, while his twin was uptight and snappy. Most likely, he was probably the one that dealt with Denise the most. How long had they played this switch-a-roo game?

Each week the flowers continued to arrive like clockwork. The Lions didn't make it to the Super Bowl, so when the regular football season ended more flowers arrived - two deliveries a week. After that, gift certificates from different department stores to shop for items for the baby.

Right after her fifth month, a handyman showed up and asked where he was supposed to do the renovations for the baby. He had already been paid and wouldn't accept anything from her. He also performed some additional renovations needed around the structure. He put in a playroom and nursery where she worked and installed cameras so she could work and watch the babies, while he took the back bedroom in her living flat and constructed a secondary nursery. Since the middle room connected the master bedroom to the nursery, he knocked out the middle room and just divided the rooms so each room would be large. She could accommodate the double cribs in her room and he also installed a sink area near the changing room.

During her sixth month doctor's appointment near the end of January, Dana arrived to find Jerome and T.J. waiting in the office for her. There were no other scheduled appointments and she suspected they might have arranged such a situation, but she was not going to cause a scene.

One was holding flowers and she couldn't tell which was Jerome. Both were comfortably dressed.

They read her mind and the one with flowers stepped closer.

"I'm Jerome. This is Tyrone, my brother."

"You're both assholes to me," Dana sneered and started to walk past them.

Tyrone grabbed her arm, but let her go when she snatched it away. "Aww, D, you can't be fucking serious."

"Don't curse!" Dana and Jerome said to him.

Dana looked at Jerome and for some reason the softness in his eyes immediately endeared her to with him. He had been her gentleman, the patient lover, while Tyrone had been the wild passionate stallion.

"How are you, Dana?" Jerome asked genuinely concerned.

"I'm fine," she answered.

Warily he stepped toward her. "We've missed you. Seriously. Tyrone kicked Denise out the house."

She gasped and looked at Tyrone.

"Not literally. J, do you have to make it sound like I'm a mean ass?"

"Quit cursing!" they said again.

Tyrone huffed. "I told her to leave in so many words and if she caused a ruckus, I would personally tell her soros about her blackmail. She didn't fight me, especially after I showed her the real marriage certificate."

"Who did I marry?" Dana asked, dying to know.

"Me," Jerome admitted. "You're legally married to me." He took out the ring that he had originally given to Denise and held it out to her. "I put on a new band with our names inscribed on the inside."

The doctor came out. "Are we okay?"

Dana took a deep breath and looked at both of them. "Yes, doctor. We're fine."

"Can we all go in?" the doctor asked.

Everyone looked at Dana for approval. "Yes," she said, accepting the ring.

Part 19

When the appointment was over, Dana allowed Jerome to drive her to the suite at the Marriott, while Tyrone followed in her car.

"How long?" Dana asked Jerome.

"Since high school. My dad remarried and got custody of me, but not Tyrone. He stayed in Florida with my real mother, who became sick and had to go to specialist in Toronto. To appease his new wife, but wanting me to be close in case my mother died, we moved to Detroit. Tyrone and I saw a lot of each other, but he didn't like school as much as I, so he dropped out. Naturally, he had a lot of time on his hands and started in on the bottle and got in a lot of trouble. Especially after our mother died. I tricked him into going to school by pretending to be me. We decided a long time ago that we could pull this off. For some reason, my brother gets a kick out of living in my life and not his own. He has his own identity in Canada, but his drinking got him into a lot of trouble and many things he couldn't do because of past mistakes. We both loved football and we competed in high school and then professionally. I'd excel at school and Tyrone would just barely get by in school unless he was me. He made a career in Canada and then after he got tired of the football thing he invested in a lot of imports and exports. Cars, items, and so forth. Not just to Canada, but Japan and Russia. He bought a shipping line right after we graduated from school and then occasional came back to just taste my life. Most of the time, I was myself. I mean the football thing was me all the way, but after a while it was tough and Tyrone didn't have an identity, yet..." He stopped at a light and looked at her. "We found we enjoyed being with one woman. We found that we were both in love with one woman. We knew there was a woman out there for both of us, but who could understand how much pleasure we derived from being with just them."

"Denise never knew?" she asked.

"She knew there was a brother, but she never asked questions about him like you did, so she never knew he was a twin. She just thought he was a bad apple, shipped to Canada with our mother and forgotten. The few times she even let us fuck her, she never knew. My father has always felt that Tyrone was the bad seed for all the trouble he was in while he was young, so my dad never talks about him or recognizes that Tyrone's alive." Jerome pulled up to the valet and they waited for Tyrone. Once inside the private elevator, Tyrone took over the story.

"Jerome fell first. We were convinced that you and Denise were one person. I spotted you in the crowds a lot at the high school games, but I just thought it was Denise. I was disguised so I never made my presence known. We never knew you were twins and the inquiries we made about Denise, even friends that went to school never mentioned you."

She felt flush. "I was a great wall flower. Most times people didn't think we were twins."

Tyrone agreed. "You were a ghost in high school. I mean we knew she had a sister, but not a twin, so Jerome actively pursued her because we both felt she was the one. Someone who loved us like that would love our…idiosyncrasies."

Dana raised a brow. "This is weird."

"For us? Yes, but for you, it's really simple," Jerome said, as they stepped off the elevator and into the suite. "We just want to please you, Dana and we're willing to do anything it takes."

Tyrone sat with her, while Jerome brought her water.

"It was getting frustrating when Denise started bi-polaring after I opened my big mouth. Of course, after that I couldn't drink a drop anymore or Jerome was going to take my tongue out personally." Tyrone chuckled bashfully.

"Then when we finally made up our mind to break it off with Denise the night before the wedding, I showed up and you're there in her dress. I mean I didn't catch on until you giggled, but after I left I told Jerome and he couldn't believe it. We were still going to break off the marriage until I snuck back up into the room through the stairs in the closet and listened to Denise's plan."

"You knew about the crawl space?" Dana asked shocked.

"I suspected something when she tried to keep the plans for the house away from me, but I found it when we also had – you know, in the closet," Tyrone reminded her. "When you pushed me back, I hit the door. After a while I came back up through the passageway and overheard what Denise wanted you to do."

She blushed profusely remembering that erotic encounter and her senses heightened even more knowing it wasn't the man who she thought it was. "So you knew all along from the get go that I wasn't Denise walking down the aisle."

"I didn't know at all about the secret passage way, or about the switch," Jerome admitted. "My dear brother never told me the heifer built the house that way, but it served as our advantage. He also didn't tell me what Denise had planned until we were in Toledo where he followed us. We confirmed all this when we both had a look at you while you were sleeping in the limousine."

Frowning suspiciously, she asked, "How did you know?"

The twins chuckled. "You had on green shoes to match ugly ass dress," Tyrone answered.

"So I slept with you originally," Dana said, pointing at Tyrone and then looking at Jerome. "And then I had a honeymoon with you?"

They both nodded, but Jerome added, "Tyrone came down to Toledo and was one of the spectators at the wedding, but you were so flustered about me knowing the truth you didn't even see him in disguise."

"That's how I got pregnant like this?" She touched her stomach.

"We're sorry," Jerome said.

Dana shook her head not at all upset. Now that everything was out in the open she almost felt a lot better. She should have been upset that she had been duped, but in return, shouldn't they be upset with her that she had pulled the same deception?

"We've done a lot to each other wrongfully, but what about Denise?"

"She's never got to know, if you don't want her to," Tyrone said. "We'd much rather whisk you and the babies off to Canada and stay in the villas we have up there for a while after you've given birth."

"Villas?" she asked confused.

Jerome rolled his eyes. "While I was busy working to get a contract and go pro, my baby brother was making millions of American dollars in import/exports."

"Millions?"

"Yes," Tyrone confirmed, nonchalantly as if it was a task people easily achieved everyday. "I may not have had a high school diploma, but business operations come natural and Jerome encouraged me to follow my nose."

"And I'd like to put on record the roll of money was his fault," Jerome stated. "Although I was clearly punished for it."

"I'm so sorry," she said apologetically.

Tyrone laughed. "Don't be, Dana, but I should apologize for demeaning our time for the sake of getting Jerome in trouble."

"He's done that a lot in our lifetime," Jerome grumbled.

These two were going to be a handful. She just knew it.

*   *   *   *   *

For the next two months Jerome had to travel, so Dana had time to familiarize herself with T.J. She discovered that even when the twins were a part they both followed the same workout schedule and tried to eat the same thing everyday including down to how many calories that they consumed. They're drive to always look alike even though they were fraternal amazed her because they really wanted this.

Tyrone was the extreme one. Temperamental and yet, awkwardly funny. Even when Dana was at her worst during the pregnancy, Tyrone somehow found patience with her, but impatience with everyone else.

They found they had similar likes. Dana enjoyed his passionate lovemaking despite her pregnancy because he was around when she really needed him sexually. He arranged to take her to Canada and marry her there unofficially at the villas he owned. Jerome attended the private ceremony and was even a witness. The ring Tyrone fashioned fit under her wedding band. Engraved on the inside was, "You were my first, last, everything, D."

Tyrone had lost his virginity with her that night under the oak tree and had told Jerome everything in detailed, but at the time, they had assumed it was Denise.

She also got to find out why Tyrone derived pleasure from living his brother's life occasionally.

"At first, it was to just mess up others because they could never tell the difference even though we were fraternal and then when I started to actually learn some things and just be Jerome, instead of my usual sarcastic behavior, it gave me a whole new insight on life." He sighed heavily. "Jerome and I had a real bad fight when he told me he was going to quit pro, 'cause I figured it was because he knew I was wanting my life back. I mean you can only live in someone else's shadow for so long before finding out that you are what you are and you need to just tell the rest of the world to f-I mean leave you alone. But he quit because he also wanted to start on his own business venture. We both have the same nose for business and pursuing it with someone we both loved is really great."

Dana could relate to that. She had lived in Denise's shadow for far too long, but the more her "twins" loved her, the more she found out that she loved herself very much.

Sometimes Jerome came home and she would spend the night in his bed. Tyrone would make himself scarce and there was never any fighting over sleeping arrangements, which Dana thought would happen. She had thoughts about handling two men at once, but the idea seemed so overwhelming, she never discussed it and they never approached it with her.

They moved her office to their home in Ann Arbor and Tyrone had a nursery quickly constructed.

By the eighth month when Jerome returned she was basically on bed rest. It was almost painfully hilarious to see

Tyrone nearly kill them trying to get to the hospital when she had false contractions.

She was confined to bed at home, while "her twins" waited on her hand and foot. A similar bed from their Florida home was designed and it was able to hold all three of them. Tyrone also redesigned the master suite so she could have her own bathroom and a bathtub similar to the one in Florida.

When nurses and doctors were around during the day, Tyrone, when he was home, stayed in the guest suite if Jerome was present. Sometimes, he did take drives to Canada to handle business, but nothing that would keep him away for over two days.

The doctor wanted her to get as close to her due date as possible, but Dana was so sick of being pregnant it had gotten to the point at her thirty-fourth week that no matter what her men did to try to make her happy, she wasn't pleased by it. Her twenty-sixth birthday was the day before her thirty-fifth week and Tyrone made her favorite, fried pork chops while Jerome made a cheesecake.

Instead of sitting in the large dining room, they sat in the back on the heated patio, because although it was nearly April, the nights were cool. They regaled her with stories of growing up. Mostly amusing her with antics they played on each other or others.

Suddenly, she asked, "What will we name them?"

"I was thinking juniors," Jerome proclaimed.

"Hey," Tyrone disputed. "I said that when she was three months."

"All right," Jerome admitted. "I had been thinking along the same lines, but we wanted you to come up with something."

Patting her stomach, she smiled tenderly giving the idea some serious thought.

The doorbell rung and Jerome went to answer it.

"Had you any names in mind?" Tyrone asked.

She looked up at him fondly and kissed him. "I was thinking...Denise?"

"No one was at the door," Jerome said, coming out on the patio again.

Tyrone heard her and sat up straight. "Denise would be a horrible name for any child. Are you trying to be funny?"

She pointed past his head at the person coming in through the back gate.

Denise, Andre and Gloria took pause at the sight of the three of them. Their mouths were wide open.

Tyrone protectively stood in front of Dana, while Jerome had to help Dana even stand up.

"There are two of them!" Gloria exclaimed and then looked back at Andre. "Did you know about this?"

"Hell naw!" Andre gasped.

"What the hell is going on?!" Denise said, looking truly appalled.

"Something you could never understand," Jerome said, putting an arm around Dana's waist, but it was also to help her stay upright as well. The weight of the babies tired her legs quickly, but she wasn't about to sit down for this.

"You're trespassing on private property," Tyrone stated flatly. "I can have you all arrested for this."

Denise pushed past all of them and bravely stood inches from Tyrone. "How long have the two of you been twins?"

"That's a rather stupid question, Denise," Jerome said.

"Look at the source," Tyrone quipped.

"You know exactly what I meant!" she snapped.

"Way before meeting you, but that's really none of your business," Jerome said.

Gloria gasped, "She's pregnant!"

"Oh Gawd!" Denise moved past Tyrone and stood face-to-face with Dana.

"She's about to explode," Andre said.

"I'll thank you kindly not to speak to my wife like that," Jerome said.

"Jerome, please," Dana said, but it wasn't Jerome she should have been scolding, because Tyrone nearly leaped across the backyard and punched Andre right in the face.

The man sprawled out on the ground at Tyrone's feet and didn't dare try to get up.

Gloria screamed and knelt to attend to her husband. "You could have killed him!" she accused.

"When? Where?!" Denise demanded.

"I'm eight months if you must know," Dana said.

Gloria gasped. "Is it Jerome's?"

"That's none of your business," Tyrone said. "Now for the second time, get the hell off my property."

Denise turned around with her usual cockiness.

"So you two have been switching places, haven't you?"

Standing between her men, Dana found the courage to stand up to her sister. Straightening her back, despite the weight that pulled her down, she snipped,

"That's neither here or there, since we did it to them, isn't that right, Denise? I wouldn't be pregnant if it weren't for you blackmailing me to switch places so you could be with your lover."

"Shut up!" Denise screamed. "You were and still are a lonely ass bitch, Dana. And you always wanted what I had! You practically seduced Jerome away from me."

"That's a lie!" Dana cried. "You practically forced me to go with him on your honeymoon."

Denise struck her across the face, and before Jerome could protect her, Dana clutched her jaw for a moment before balling her own fists and giving Denise a one-two punch to her jaw and then nose.

Denise fell out to the ground, passed out cold with the imprint of Dana's diamond ring imprinted on her face.

"Bitch!" Gloria sneered at Dana, standing up.

"I don't know why you're calling me a bitch," Dana said, leaning again on Jerome as a sharp pain struck her backside.

"She's the one sleeping with your husband."

Gloria gasped and looked at the guilty Andre who tried to defend himself by saying, "Baby, she seduced me!"

His wife started wildly kicking him with her high shoes, while he still lay on the ground.

Dana would have laughed if she was not in the midst of the most excruciating pain in her lower abdomen and backside.

"Oh Jesus!" Tyrone said, walking over to Dana and seeing the fluid streaming down her leg.

Jerome scooped her up and headed to the hospital. After Tyrone successfully removed everyone off their property, he followed with her things and called the doctor and the hospital to make sure all the arrangements they had prepared for in advance were in place.

Dana wanted to scream, but instead she bit her lip. Jerome patiently coached her on the way there in the car and once they were in their private room, she had both of their support during the labor.

Jerome was the more patient one and better coach. Tyrone actually went quite pale as she began to push his son out into the world, but he stayed conscious and was able to cut the cord. When the next one came, Jerome cut the cord.

Tyrone kissed her brow. "You did it, D. We're so proud of you."

Jerome gave her a fat sloppy proud kiss. Dana looked at their happy faces and knew this was what she wanted – both of them. She wasn't a 'lonely ass bitch' anymore and would never be again.

Yet, she couldn't even speak. It felt as if all her energy was pouring out of her body all of a sudden.

"Nurse, bring me some more gauze," the doctor ordered.

"What's wrong?" Tyrone said.

The staff was hastily moving around the room to give the doctor whatever he barked out.

"It's not stopping. She's hemorrhaging," the doctor said. "Get the surgeon in here!"

"Dana!" Jerome called her, but he sounded like he was so far away even though his face was inches from her own.

"The...babies..." she forced out.

"They're fine," Tyrone assured her. "Please, D, stay with us."

"I love you both," she whispered before she let the blackness transport her to a pain free place.

Part 20

Three months. That was the recovery time. Even after that she had to take it easy, but in the Canadian villa Tyrone owned, it was like spending every day at a spa. She was pampered to death. Along with a weight and workout coach, she was massaged daily and treated like a queen.

In the villa, Jerome and Tyrone could be present all the time together. The staff was all employed by Tyrone and were highly paid and entrusted to keep their mouths shut.

Jerome found Dana a great assistant to keep her business going, while she was in Canada. Her business was moved back into Dana's old home, so they could close off the Ann Arbor home until Dana decided to come back.

Both men took brief paternity leaves from work and after the DNA results came in, they were able to place their names of their son's birth records.

It was quite amusing because they had cut the right child's cord. Jerome had the scissors bronzed and on the babies fourth months, Tyrone had their first shoes bronzed.

By that time, Dana was back to her normal size and health except she was a little fuller in the chest area. Jerome and Tyrone had been patient and loving and never pressured her for sex. Having them both separately had been a sort of nuisance and she thought about it long and hard before she came to her own decision to take matters in her own hands.

When they were having dinner a month after the first wedding anniversary, Jerome was rattling off about getting back to work in the states and their living arrangements.

"What's on your mind, Dana?" Tyrone asked, who had been watching her.

She could tell he was horny and she bet if she passed gas he would he think that was a turn on. Snickering at this thought, she said, "I was thinking before we get back to work, I think we should take a trip. I'm sure Marva and John will be able to handle the boys for a couple of days."

Marva and John were the adorable French couple that served as nanny and security for the children. Married, they had never had children of their own and doted on Ty and Jay day and night.

"I think that's a great idea," Tyrone quickly said.

"We can leave in the morning."

"It's rather sudden, isn't it," Jerome said.

"Nope," Tyrone and Dana said together.

Dana giggled, knowing what Tyrone's salacious thoughts were up to.

"I could get us a yacht by tomorrow morning," Tyrone said, easily as if he were just going to the grocery store for a loaf of bread. "It wouldn't be too difficult to get a two bedroom."

"With a private crew?" Jerome asked.

"Yes."

"I wouldn't need my own room," she said, assuming that Tyrone and Jerome would share to give her some privacy.

Both men looked at her.

"Well, Dana, we wouldn't want you to share, if you didn't want to," Jerome said.

"I wouldn't mind sharing with the two of you."

Tyrone leaned forward. "You mean share us in one night, Dana."

Blushing, she nodded.

"Are you sure?" Jerome asked. "We don't want you to do anything you don't want to do."

"I love you, both," she said adamantly.

"I'll get the bath," Jerome said, getting up from the table.

"I'll get the arrangements for tomorrow and join you in a few." Tyrone kissed her briefly and left the room.

"I'll check the boys." She ordered the table be cleaned off and the staff to leave them alone for the rest of the night. Once she checked her beautiful children, she went over to where Jerome was starting a bath in the large tub, which was similar to the one in Florida as well.

She started to undress, but he stopped her and took over, kissing every inch of skin he revealed. Dana reveled in his wonderful lips. He dropped to his knees to suck her clit, lick voraciously around her labia and then lick her moist cavern until she orgasmed in his mouth. She moved to her knees in the candle lit bathroom to undress him. He sat on the edge of the tub as she knelt to pull his pants and shoes off. Once she removed his clothes, she kissed up his calf and then both inner thighs. Licking his swelling dark orbs, loving the velvety feel of them on her tongue, she languished around his base before moving up to feel him grow in her mouth. Jerome clutched the edge of the tub enjoying every moment her mouth suckled him to completion. They stopped the warm water and got in the bath together.

First, Jerome stood while she soaped him up and washed him from head to toe. Just as he was being rinsed off, Tyrone appeared at the doorway and began to undress. A little apprehensive of being able to handle two men at once, she smiled assuredly at him as he stepped in the water with them.

Dana was in the middle of the two of them and Jerome sat on the edge of the tub, while Dana washed Tyrone from head to foot. He kissed her passionately throughout, his member was hard and she paid extra attention, first laving it with her tongue and then washing it with soap. When she rinsed it off, she sucked him until his essence burst forth down her throat.

They made her stand in the middle of the tub, while Jerome took the front and Tyrone took the back. They didn't miss an inch and where the washcloth couldn't go, their hands and fingers touched. She felt like the queen of the world as she was given special attention with their mouths from the front and the back as they rinsed her off.

Tyrone scooped her up and carried her to the bedroom, which had been also lit with candles. She let him dry her off before she crawled up on the large bed and pulled him down in her arms. Their lips were entwined and their tongues danced a passionate tango that incited their lust and wantonness. Tyrone entered easily and she came instantly around his dick.

Jerome came over to the other side of the bed and leaned down to kiss her. He was the slower kisser and loved to massage her breast while they kissed upside down as Tyrone plunged repeatedly into her.

Moving down her neck and then to her breast, Jerome gave each nipple special attention, but then concentrated on her right, while Tyrone leaned over and concentrated on her left.

Dana gasped passionately at the dual sensation of having her nipples stimulated by similar mouths. What woman had never dreamed of having something like this?

Her hands reached up to grab Jerome's shaft to give him an anvil stroke with her hands. The sensation brought him fully erect and he had to stop his own titillation of her body too consumed with what she was doing to his manhood.

"Oh damn, woman," he hissed.

The curse rule was thrown out in bed and she giggled seductively as he moved up and she let him fuck her mouth, while Tyrone pounded her to ecstasy.

She was enjoying every second and knew the night wasn't nearly over. They took turns in different positions making full use of their humongous bed. Since both men had come earlier, they're stamina kept them strong and hard until the pentacle.

Dana straddled Jerome while vivaciously sucking Tyrone deep in her mouth. Tyrone was close. She could feel the pulse in his dick and his balls had drawn up so tight, she knew she was affecting him greatly, especially since her finger had easily slipped up his ass and was fondling his prostate. Tyrone was stuttering like he usually did and Dana was delighting in her power over these two men.

They needed her. They loved her. They would give her the world on a silver platter and she would always be their first love and the mother of their children.

"N-Not yet, D," Tyrone pleaded. "Please."

She released him reluctantly and he moved behind her, over Jerome's legs to insert himself into her anus. Jerome's mouth was buried in her chest as he enjoyed the fullness of her breast and when he felt his brother's dick sliding against the thin skin that separated her two chasms, he looked up at her and cupped her face.

"We love you, D," he whispered.

She was in pure bliss as they began to move against each other. Tyrone massaged her left breast while he nibbled on her back and whispered sweet words of love, wanton, and forever his. Jerome's hands attacked her right breast and he kissed her neck, cheeks and then lips.

Their moans of gratification mingled together and as Dana began to slowly orgasm it felt like a great Tsunami wave enveloping her body and her innards quivered, drawing both men tighter and manipulating them to explode with her.

Dana collapsed on Jerome's chest panting heavily. Tyrone lay on her back, but restrained his full weight.

She wasn't lonely anymore. She was loved.

The End

If you enjoyed this story and would like to make a $5 donation to support this author's endeavors, please go to the bottom of the following website and click "Donation."

http://SylviaHubbard.com

For your donation, you'll receive a free book by mail from this author.

To read more of this author's work, please check out her website:
http://SylviaHubbard.homestead.com

To order the paperback of this book, go to:

http://lulu.com/SylviaHubbard

Or order free short stories from this author at:

http://Hubbooks.homestead.com

stealing innocence by Sylvia Hubbard

Tying a man down to get what she wants leads to sweet pay back!

Kimberly could not believe what her uncle wanted her to do. In order to keep the inheritance of her husband's, her uncle wanted her to get pregnant. Yet, when Hawthorne dies unexpectedly, Uncle Charles kidnaps a man who resembles Kimberly's decease husband, ties him to a bed, and orders Kimberly to rape the man until she is pregnant. Uncle Charles would kill him, after the deed was done so no one would ever know the truth. Having no choice in the matter, Kimberly faces the exquisite dark body of man and in her innocence, prepares herself to steal his seed.

Surly, mean tempered Jaelen can't believe someone had the nerve to tie him to the bed. When his cold eyes fall on the beautiful, angelic Kimberly and he realizes her intentions, he vows to escape and get revenge if it takes the rest of his life.

AVAILABLE NOW!

http://lulu.com/SylviaHubbard

Drawing the Line

by Sylvia Hubbard

erotic/suspense with three times the excitement!

Overview:

Shane needs money to get away from her money hungry aunt. Her boss, Andrew and his brother, Paul, offer her "ultimate pleasure" if she gives them the child they need in order to keep a company they've worked hard to make successful. She accepts their offer, but realizes she has trouble drawing the line in her feelings for her handsome boss.

Yet, the bond that draws them all together is soon put to the test when Shane comes up missing amidst a chemical company land scandal she was investigating.

Andrew and Paul hope they find Shane in time before she loses the baby.

Available soon @ http://SylviaHubbard.com

Reader's Check List

(mark off when you have read the works by this author)

Other novels by this author:

- ❑ Dreams of Reality*
- ❑ Stone's Revenge*
- ❑ Stealing Innocence +
- ❑ Stealing Innocence 2: The Ravishment +
- ❑ Mistaken Identity
- ❑ Road to Freedom
- ❑ Deceptive Nights
- ❑ Teach Me To Love +

Other novellas by this author:

- ❑ Cabin Fever +
- ❑ Red Heart +
- ❑ Baby Doll +

Other short stories

- ❑ How to Meet and Marry in 24 Hours
- ❑ Country Road
- ❑ Boom! Boom! Boom!
- ❑ Silent Lynx +

Works in progress:

- ❑ Other Side of Love +
- ❑ Drawing the Line
- ❑ Dark Façade +
- ❑ Stealing Innocence III: Lethal Heart +
- ❑ King's Paradise+

* Available on Amazon.com   + Part of Heart of Detroit Series

About this author:

Detroit Native, Sylvia Hubbard, is a diehard romance/suspense author. In 2005, Sylvia Hubbard was the recipient of The Detroit City Council's Spirit of Detroit Award for her efforts in Detroit's literary community, voted Romance Book Cafe favorite author and her book Stone's Revenge was voted best African-American Mystery by Mojolist.com. The Author is also founder of Motown Writers Network, which offers literary education and events in Detroit, Editor In Chief of The Essence of Motown Literary Magazine and speaks on Internet Marketing and Promotions for Writers and Authors.

She resides in Detroit as a divorced mother of three. She writes a blog called How To Love A Black Woman, which is described as her manual for loving her, and speaks on Creative Intimacy for couples.

Related Links:

http://MotownWriters.com

http://LoveABlackWoman.blogspot.com

http://MotownRomance.blogspot.com

CPSIA information can be obtained at www.ICGtesting.com
Printed in the USA
LVOW050237300612

288304LV00002B/139/A